D1714068

STRIPPING ASJIAH II

WRITTEN BY SA'RESE ⌊BLOOD MONEY⌋

Library of Congress Control Number: In publication data
Copyright: © 2011 by La' Femme Fatale' Productions
ISBN 13: 9780983393252
Cover Design: Davida Baldwin Oddball Dsgn
Edited by: Michelle West
Author: Sa'Rese
Interior: Write on Promotions

Published by:
La' Femme Fatale' Productions
9900 Greenbelt Road
Suite E333
Lanham, Maryland 20706
WWW.LFFPUBLISHING.COM

Printed in Canada

Dedication

Everything I do, everything that I am and everything that I'll ever be, I owe it all to you. Sometimes I look in the mirror and see your reflection, or I hear your voice when I speak, sometimes it's something as small as my mannerisms that remind me of you. I don't know if I will ever be able to accept your absence, because to me; to us, you are still here. You are the air that I breathe, the smile on my face, and the light in my eyes. You are my hope for tomorrow and my reason for living. If I accomplish nothing else in life, my dream is to be half of the woman you were and still are to me. I love you.

Sometimes I feel like I'm seeing the world through your eyes. Like my heart isn't my own but yours as well. You have taught me not to run from fear, but to embrace it. To love those who hate me and to learn to forgive those who have caused me pain. Unconsciously it seems that my love for you has allowed you to heal although at times I feel like it's killing me, but if I can bring you joy, that's all that matters to me. There's so much more I can say, just know that if I had it to do all over again, I would still choose you. You're my dad, my father, my friend, and I love you.

Acknowledgements

Leave it to me to make writing my acknowledgements difficult. I've rewrote this a million times and the more I thought about it, the shorter my list became. There were some people who I acknowledged and thanked in Stripping Asjiah that didn't deserve it. I found myself being grateful to people who I was "acquainted" with but had never read one line, came out to an open mic, or even purchased the book, people I had known for years but didn't "know" shit about me, those who were only around for good times but never there to grind it out and hold me down during the bad. I'm not going to do that with this one. I've never been one to run with a lot of people so those I kept close to me, I felt like they deserved to be there, like they understood me, those were the ones I confided in, that I shared my story with, but I've come to realize that no matter how much I told them, no matter how good of a friend I was or tried to be, they still didn't get me.

You can paint a picture for millions of people hoping that they will all see the same thing you do but everyone is going to formulate their own opinion, everyone's depiction of the portrait is going to be different and if I spent my days worrying about what people had to say, about what they thought, constantly living for the validation of others, I wouldn't get too far. So no matter how small my circle gets, I'd rather be at the top with those who I know are "true friends" versus those who only endured the climb just to push me off.

Now that I got that out of the way, first and foremost I need to give all thanks to God who is the head of my life. In times when I curse you, question you, or feel as if you have abandoned me, I know those are the times when you are with me the most. I would not be where I am today if it weren't for you holding my hand and walking with me continuously throughout this journey I call life. I am forever thankful for everything you've done and continue to do for me. This past year has been a test for me on various levels and if it weren't for your grace and mercy, I wouldn't have made it. I only ask that you will continue to hold my hand and allow me to be a better woman than I am right now, than I was yesterday, or that I will be tomorrow.

To my extended family at Cover Me Presents, Black Tuesday, Art of Storytelling and Laughing and Lounging...thank you for allowing me to touch the mic.

To Lauren Manney...words can't express how much you mean to me. You accepted me into your heart and have loved me unconditionally for the past nine years. When I need someone to talk to, no matter the time or the day, I know I can call on you. I will always love you no matter what. You will always be like a mother to me.

Mommy Sharon you are an amazing woman and I've never had someone care so much about me to not have met me in person. You believe that I'm a phenomenon, a brilliant force to reckon with; at times I've found myself staring at my reflection trying to make sure it's me that you're referring to. I love you and for seeing a part of me that is often shaded by the darkness in the world. My heart will always be in California.

My heart and soul; Peanut, you've had my heart since the day you were born and although I can't be with you everyday like I want to, know that your "Tee-tee" is always thinking of you. If I could give you the world, I would. You are the reason I live. If you know nothing else in life, know that I would do ANYTHING for you and it was never my intentions to be absent from your life. A lot of times people do things out of spite and innocent people become casualties of their malice, I don't expect you to understand but hopefully one day soon things will get better. I love you immensely. To my brother; I feel like the world has pushed and pulled us in so many directions, torn us into so many pieces that at times we forget how to put ourselves back together. It hurts that we aren't the way we once were but I've learned to remove myself from situations that aren't healthy for me, no matter the person or the circumstance. We share a bond that no one else in this world can break, at the end of it all; you will always be my big brother, my Angel, my dark knight. I love you madly.

To Jay, where do I start? Crazy how things have played out for us thus far, looking back on it all, I wouldn't change a thing. There are so many things I want to say to you but I feel like I'm going to have a lifetime to do it. Thank you for being my better half. Thank you for talking me through things when I don't always see both sides of a situation, for entertaining and listening to all my crazy ideas and thoughts, for understanding my vision and letting me be who I am. You are so many things that I'm not and I love you for that. At times your intellect frightens me, in a good way being that you view the world so differently than I do so that grants you the ability to open my eyes to things they would've remained closed to. Thank you for making me smile in times that I want to cry, thank you for pushing me to get out of my comfort zone and daring me to be great, for allowing me to stand on my own and believing that I can do it. Thank you for "time out" although I don't like it, I understand why you do it. Thank you for being patient (I know I can be a lot to deal with sometimes), for being understanding and for loving me unconditionally. If you could pull the stars out of the sky, I know you would, in the meantime I'll take one of those cards. (Ah! It's fairy tale love)

Most importantly, thank you to the fan base that has grown due to the success of Stripping Asjiah. This book has taken on a life of it's own that I wasn't expecting. To everyone out in Vacaville, Ca; thank you for all your support. Rootz, Benny, Mike, my body guard Raheim, Dr. Omara, and to everyone in Talladega Al; T-Mo, Infamous, Papa, Eric, Plat. If there is anyone I didn't name, blame my mind and not my heart. All of you have read between the lines and fell in love with the person behind the words, not just the words themselves. Urban literature is a tough genre to compete in especially when you are a first time author, so I would like to personally thank all of those who purchased my book and wrote reviews for it, blogged about it or came out to a signing. Your support is greatly appreciated. I promised to deliver a sequel that would top my first one and I hope you enjoy it. I'm sorry it took so long. Stay tuned because there is so much more to come.

Sa'Rese

From the beginning we were set up to fail
The odds stacked against us-
Fast cash, drugs, and sex the perfect recipe to tempt us.
God had abandoned us
Stranded us in this hell we called life-
He showed us first hand marriage wasn't shit when he
allowed our father to kill his wife.
But the devil said he'd save us
So to him we pledged our allegiance-
Not knowing it would cost me my son and my brother his
freedom.

Family; we don't need'em
Like vultures they just wanted to pick our bones-
Kick us when we're down
Point fingers
And throw stones-
Out the windows of their glass houses built with betrayal
and lies-
Threatening to shatter around them; exposing years of
scandal and incestuous ties.
Friends had turned to enemies leaving us with no one to
trust-
Back to back we stood together as demons surrounded us.
Our eyes are dark
Hearts cold from the things that have happened
There's no room for fear inside us
All emotions are absent.

We've been stripped of everything; what more could you
take from me?
Fuck it, you can have it all
To us
It's just
Blood Money.
Asjiah Cappelli

Preface

"Don't forget to remind your parents about the Science Fair tomorrow!"

The anxious second graders gathered their book bags and homework assignments as they lined up by the door and waited for the bell.

"Mr. Donnelly, can I help you feed Strawberry?"

"Of course you can." Mr. Donnelly clapped the erasers together sending dust flying all over his glasses.

Asjiah laughed as chalk covered her teacher's face.

"Seems like I'm making quite the mess doesn't it?" Retrieving a Kleenex from the box on his desk; he wiped off his lenses and said goodbye to the students just as the bell was ringing.

"Okay, now let us visit our friend shall we?" Mr. Donnelly gently grabbed Asjiah by the hand and led her over to the tank that held the massive boa constrictor they affectionately called Strawberry. Bright red splotches decorated the serpents cream colored body which coiled intricately around the glass case.

"Remember, drop the mouse on the opposite end and not directly in front of Strawberry okay Asjiah?"

"Okay." Asjiah took the cover off the small box which contained a tiny, albino mouse.

"Ooh can I watch?" Angel appeared outside of the door just as his sister was getting ready to feed the snake.

"Well hello there Angel, come right in."

Angel was in Mr. Donnelly's class during his second grade year and often came to pay his favorite Science teacher visits during the day.

Angel dropped his backpack next to the door and joined his sister. They both watched in silence as she placed the un-expecting mouse next to the predator.

At first Strawberry seemed unaware of the rodent but it didn't take long before it began to flicker its tongue and sense out its prey.

"Do you remember why Strawberry uses her tongue to detect the mouse?"

"Because..."

"Shhh! Not you Angel, he asked me!" Asjiah placed her hand over her brother's mouth to silence his outburst.

"Because that's how they smell."

"Good job Asjiah."

Delighted by her answer, she turned to her brother and grinned exposing small spaces in her gums that once held two teeth.

"I was going to say the same thing." Angel playfully pushed her as he went to retrieve his things.

"Come on A' we have to go, mommy should be out front waiting for us."

"Thank you Mr. Donnelly!" The pair gathered their book bags and headed out the door.

"You two are very welcome, and don't forget about the fair tomorrow."

Mr. Donnelly smiled as the two siblings scurried off unaware of the troubles that lay before them.

Sean sat inside the black C-class Mercedes tapping the steering wheel as he waited for his kids to get out of school. Since him and Jai split up; she had informed the principle not to allow the children to leave with anyone else but her. He felt like a spectator, an observer watching his life play out behind a two-way mirror.

Just as he was beginning to get agitated thinking about the situation he saw his baby girl emerge followed by her brother; "My babies."

It seemed like eternity had passed since the last time he had seen them, when in reality it had only been a month. Angel was getting so big and Asjiah was as cute as ever. Her pigtails playfully bounced up and down as she played hop scotch next to her brother.

"Quit staring and go get them." Sandra noisily popped her gum in the passenger seat as she rolled her eyes in annoyance.

Sean unlocked the door and stepped out of the car just as his wife's cherry BMW pulled into the parking lot.

"Is that her?" Suddenly interested, Sandra sat up in her seat as she watched the kids run over and hug who appeared to be their mother.

This was her first time actually seeing Jai in person. She had seen pictures of her before but they clearly did her no justice, she was gorgeous; maybe 5'3, petite, probably a size three at the most, with flawless, Hershey kissed skin and a body worthy of attention. Her hair lay between her shoulder blades which moved gracefully each time the wind blew.

"Yeah, that's Jai," Sean watched his wife play with the kids and his anger towards her began to resurface. She was able to help them with homework, eat dinner with them, hear about all the things that had happened during school and throughout their days and he had to stand on the sidelines. She was stealing everything from him; robbing him of a family that he helped create. He gulped down the rest of his beer before slamming the door and walking towards the school.

"Hey baby girl," Sean approached Asjiah with his arms outstretched.

Dropping her book bag, she ran into her father's arms, "Daddy!"

"Hey munchkin," Sean brushed his daughter's curls out her face and kissed her cheek.

"I've missed you so much."

"Daddy I have a Science fair tomorrow. Are you going to come?" Asjiah placed her tiny hands on each side of her father's face so that he was looking directly at her.

"Now that you're back you can help me make my Volcano. Mommy said she would do it but I know yours would be better." The seven-year old giggled as she looked back at her mother.

Seeing him interact with them was making her uncomfortable.

"What are you doing here Sean?"

Dusting his hands off on his jeans he looked up at his wife. "I just wanted to see my kids Jai."

"Your kids,"

"Yes my kids." Sean walked closer turning his attention to his son.

"Angel, how you been man? How's my little boy doing?"

Startled by his father's voice, Angel stood still.

"You're getting so big; you look just like your mother. What's wrong, you don't want to give your pops a hug?"

"Leave him alone Sean."

"What Jai?" He playfully nudged Angel in the head putting his fists up pretending to spar with the young child.

"Have you been helping Mommy around the house while I was gone?"

"Yes sir. I also kicked a home run during kickball today and my class beat Mr. Miller's!" Angel began to ease up a little as he relived his victory during recess.

"That's really good. When I come home you'll have to show me the move you did."

"When *are* you coming home Daddy?" Asjiah's blue eyes twinkled as she looked at her father and waited for him to respond.

"Well…"

"Angel, take your sister and get in the car. Mommy and Daddy have to talk now."

"But Mom, I wanted to tell dad about the frogs we got in Science class today."

"Now Angel,"

Angel obediently did what his mother asked as he looked back at his father one last time before taking Asjiah's hand and leading her to the car.

Even with the window rolled down Sandra couldn't hear what was being said. She stepped out the car and tried to get closer to the action.

"I have no problem with you seeing your kids Sean, but not like this. They didn't know you were coming, you scared them and you smell like you've been drinking."

"I had one beer, but I'm not drunk." Sean put his hand up to his eyes and staggered backwards in an attempt to shield the sun from his face.

"You need to get yourself together, and then we can talk about you possibly coming over to see them."

"Who the fuck are you to tell me that I can *possibly* see *my* kids?"

Jai brushed off her Donna Karan slacks and placed her hands on her hips.

"First of all, you mean *our* kids and you're in no condition to be around them right now. So like I said, until you get your shit together; don't come around them."

"Okay, okay, look Jai, I'm sorry. This is getting out of hand and I can understand if you are mad at me but I never meant to hurt you." Sean placed his hands around his wife's waist as he tried to calm her down.

Jai stared back into his sky blue eyes and for a moment, she lost herself. He was dressed in dark blue Levi's, wheat Timberlands, and a crisp white v-neck t-shirt. A diamond stud kissed his left earlobe and his dog tags were hanging around his neck.

He smelled of Hugo Boss; the same fragrance that used to cover her skin after they finished making love. He resembled the Sean she fell in love with, the man she married. *Could* everything go back to normal?

Up until today, the kids thought their father was away on field duty with the Army. They were used to him going away for weeks at a time so they didn't question her story. Now she would have to explain to them what he was doing back and why daddy hadn't come home.

"Give me another chance Jai, I promise I will make everything up to you." Sean ran his fingers through her hair and he could feel the tension between them begin to subside. "We can all get away; take the kids somewhere for the weekend, maybe drive up to Santa Monica. What do you think?"

"Are mommy and daddy fighting again?"
"It's okay A', they're just talking." Angel didn't know what was going on either but he knew that he couldn't allow his sister to see that he was just as confused as she was.
"So what are you going to make for the Science fair?"
"Huh?"
"The Science fair silly, it starts tomorrow."
"Oh yeah…"
Angel listened as she began to ramble about the volcano that she was planning to build. He was glad that he was able to distract her even though his thoughts still remained outside with their mother.

Sandra was staring at Jai with daggers in her eyes. She felt used, like a pawn in this chess game he was playing to get his queen back. She was the reason they had split in the first place, she was the other woman. He told her that his marriage was over; that he would leave Jai for her and until she saw her, she thought he was being truthful.

Looking at them together now, there was no way he was going to leave her. You had to be a fool to leave a woman like that.

Sandra wasn't ugly but she knew she couldn't hold a candle to Jai, not even on her bad days. Jai was small and in shape; Sandra was heavier and average. It wasn't only her looks but they were a family, they had two beautiful children, what could she offer him to compete with that?

He was going to leave her, throw her out with the garbage because that's what she was to him; trash. Unless…unless she could convince him that she had something just as valuable to offer.

It wasn't like they hadn't been having unprotected sex so her claiming to be pregnant wouldn't be too far fetched. She only needed to pretend long enough to get him to leave Jai then right at the moment he would start asking questions; she would begin to complain of cramps, headaches, fatigue, and fake a miscarriage.

She had allowed Sean to sell her a dream that she couldn't afford to buy. She just had to figure out a way to get rid of Cinderella so she could have her happily ever after.

"I don't know Sean, I mean I don't want to agree to this and then something happens again. I don't want to mislead the children. If you are going to be in our lives then you need to leave all that other shit alone and make sure that we are really what you want."

"But you are baby," Sean tilted Jai's chin and softly kissed her on the lips. He had forgotten what it was like to feel her, to hold her; this was the way things were supposed to be.

"Sean, it's time to go!"

The entire time they had been talking Jai didn't notice the woman standing by her husband's car. She backed away from him and turned her attention towards the female who was yelling his name.

"And who the fuck is that?"

Seeing that she had angered Jai, Sandra smiled and waived at her.

"Oh hell no," Taking her Chanel hoops out her ear, Jai began to walk towards the Mercedes.

"Jai, calm down, she's nobody. The kids are in the car, do you really want to do this here, in front of them?"

"Nobody; is that the bitch you've been cheating on me with? You fucked up our family for that homely looking broad?" Jai couldn't believe she had allowed him to sweet talk her into thinking everything could be fixed, that everything could be okay.

"Jai, I know what this may look like. But I promise you babe, it's over. She only came up here with me because I asked her to."

"Fuck you," Swatting his hands off her waist she backed away from him.

"Fuck you and that bitch. You thought you were going to come up here, take my kids, and have my babies around another woman? You have got to be out of your fucking mind!" Jai spun around on her heels and began to walk towards her car.

"You let her know I'll catch up with her ass. Then again, never mind, she isn't worth it. You can have her." Jai smoothed her hair, fixed her blouse and got inside the BMW.

"Kids, say bye to your father."

"Bye dad." Ignorant to what had just happened; the children complied.

"Jai wait!"

He wanted to chase after her. He wanted to tell her that he meant everything he had just told her but there was no way she would believe him now.

He felt his heart shatter, it was as if his soul left his body and he was being forced to watch his life unravel before him.

In that moment, on that day, Sean felt as if he died right there in the parking lot of Stillwell Elementary as he looked at his baby girl wave bye to him out the back window. He was empty, defeated. He was so close; so close to having his life back.

"Jai!"

His chest was caving in, he couldn't breathe. It was like his ribs were forming a steel cage around his heart as it slowly turned to stone. Tears began to roll down his face as he watched helplessly while his family drove away.

"Well that didn't go as planned now did it?" A devilish grin played across Sandra's lips as she looked at the humility that covered Sean's face.

"Get out of my car." His voice was calm and steady as the soft click of the locks gave Sandra her cue to exit.

"What?" She knew he was mad but he was over reacting by trying to kick her out of the car. They were all the way on the opposite side of town. It would take her at least two hours to get home.

The engine purred to life as he stared through the windshield. "I said get out."

"Sean, it's not that serious."

Was he crying? In all the months that she knew him, she had never seen him cry but in the brief time he was talking to Jai she was able to evoke such strong emotions out of him. She hated her. She despised Jai for making her seem so insignificant. He had never displayed these type of feelings for her; yet this hoe could prance up here in her $50,000 car, expensive jewelry, and instantly make this nigga bitch up without even trying. It was evident that he loved Jai; in a way that she knew he would never love her.

"Quit playing and let's go." Trying to shake her thoughts; Sandra ignored him and continued to sit comfortably in the leather seat.

Sean's jaw clenched and his cheeks became flushed as he turned to her.

"Get the fuck out of my car. Don't make me tell you again."

There was something about his eyes that frightened her. They were lifeless. For a moment, she stared back at him and tried to find remnants of the person that was just smiling and hugging his wife but no one was there. It was as if she was looking through an empty window. She was afraid what might happen if she continued to challenge him, so she opened the passenger door and stepped out of the car. Before she could say anything, he pulled off leaving her in a cloud of smoke.

"Okay, let's get inside so you guys can do your homework." Jai gathered the groceries along with her briefcase as she followed behind her kids into the house.

"Hi Bear." Jai affectionately greeted the Rottweiler who was waiting obediently by the patio door.

"Outside, does mommy's baby have to go outside?" Bear lovingly licked her hand a few times before opting to go relieve himself.

"Mommy can you make strawberry shortcake?" Angel licked his lips as if he could taste the sweet dessert already.

"Only if you two do your homework and get all of the answers correct."

"What if I miss one question?" Angel sat down at the table and began unpacking his book bag.

"What if I miss one too?" Climbing up into her chair, Asjiah mimicked her brother.

"You two are too much. I'll be back; I left my bag in the car."

Angel and Asjiah were too busy laughing and playing with each other to hear what their mother said.

Unlocking the doors on the BMW she grabbed her Louis Vuitton bag off the backseat. As she closed the door she noticed Sean's black Mercedes parked on the corner of the cul de sac.

Their eyes met and she replayed the things he said to her at the school and wanted desperately to believe him but how could she when he had that woman with him? He was making a mockery out of her, out of their marriage. After what seemed like hours she turned, walked back in the house, and set the alarm.

Sean's hands were beginning to turn red as he gripped the steering wheel.

"I should be in that house, my house; with my family. Not out here on the street like some stray dog and I would've been if it wasn't for that bitch Sandra."

"Sandra."

The leather started to make grinding noises underneath his palms as he imagined his hands around her throat. He wanted her to choke on the words she had so viciously spewed from her mouth. He wanted her to know what it felt like to be hurt, to feel pain; she needed to experience the sorrow that was eating away at his heart.

Sean put the car in reverse as his house slowly faded into the rearview. He would get back what he lost no matter the cost or what he had to do to get it.

STRIPPING

ASJIAH

II

Blood Money

Chapter One

It's raining; hard.

The intensity of the raindrops makes it difficult to hear anything else, including her thoughts. She could almost time the lightening. The thunder rumbles through the sky, the rain pours heavily,

Then five...four...three...two...one...

She couldn't open her eyes but she could see the flash of light as it illuminated behind closed eyelids.

Each drop seemed to have its own destination. Some of them never touched, some ran together and then split apart. But all of them seemed to be racing to get out of the clouds, racing to get as far from heaven as possible. And in a way that's how she felt, as if she had fallen out of God's good graces.

She was moving too fast, got involved in all the wrong shit, and once she began to fall she couldn't stop until ultimately, like the raindrops, she fell to the ground.

Too caught up in the allure of things it seemed as if everybody wanted her and even if she didn't want them, she wanted what they could do for her in that moment. The way they made her feel, the way they touched her, looked at her; but where were all those people now? *Where the hell was she*?

She couldn't tell if she was alive or somewhere in purgatory awaiting either the Lord's angels to rescue her or Satan's minions to come carry her off to the depths of hell. At this point, she would willingly welcome the flames of Lucifer's fiery pit verses what she was feeling right now.

BY SA'RESE

She was certain her ribs were broken, her head was pounding and it felt as if her brain was being squeezed by a vice. She felt wet. Like she was laying in something, whatever it was she knew it wasn't water; it smelled metallic. Could it be blood?

Her lips felt swollen, maybe even busted.

What the hell happened?

Why couldn't she remember anything? How long had she been here?

The rain stopped for a moment and the lightening flashed again. The silhouette of a person danced behind her swollen eyes. Scared, her voice shook as she called out only for silence to answer.

"Who, whose there; hello?"

It was quiet, too quiet.

"Is someone in here?"

She waited for a few minutes then realized that her mind must've been playing tricks on her so she laid back down. Exhaustion rushed over her and she felt as though she was crashing; as if she was coming off of a high too fast. She tried to open her eyes again but to no avail. *Was she blind?*

"Ah!"

A sharp pain rushed through her pelvis, across her lower back, then down to her vagina causing her to urinate on herself. It burned, something was wrong. What happened to her? She felt like she had been beaten with aluminum baseball bats, her entire body ached.

Thunder rattled the window and it began to rain again. Trying to get up she maneuvered her way through the darkness but with each move she made, pain paralyzed her and demanded that she be still.

STRIPPING ASJIAH

Her hands immediately began to touch her body and fear rushed through her as she realized she didn't have any clothes on. Why was she naked? This couldn't be real. Was she dreaming?

She stepped on what she believed to be pants, then a jacket; did these clothes belong to her? She could hear the constant humming of a toilet and the dripping of a faucet. As she approached what she hoped to be the bathroom her fingers ran across a light switch and the bright glow caused her head to hurt even more. Banging her knee against the sink, she fumbled around the vanity trying to position her self in front of it.

"Open your eyes. Please open your eyes." Pleading with God she hoped he would allow her to awake although she was certain she had already been condemned to hell.

Chapter Two

"Mmm…right there, right there." Danielle grinded her hips against his face as she put her hand on his head and guided him to her spot.

Placing his finger inside of her, Mike continued to suck on her clit causing her to moan in ecstasy while he simultaneously massaged her walls.

Pinching her nipples, she squeezed and played with her breast as his tongue dived deeper and deeper into her ocean.

"Ahh…"

Smiling Mike wiped his mouth and watched as her fountain erupted and she squirted all over the sheets.

She tossed a condom towards him, spread her legs, and waited for him to ravage her. Danielle's voice was low and ragged as she tried to catch her breath.

"Fuck me."

Submitting to her request he willingly obliged, "Is this what you wanted?"

Strands of auburn hair fell into her face as her head banged against the headboard. She smiled wickedly as she traced the outside of his lips before placing her toes in his mouth.

"Yes."

Mike held her waist tightly, relishing in the sight of the faces he was causing her to make.

Lightening flashed behind the curtains catching their bodies in a seductive dance as they climaxed.

"Whew," Mike dismounted and collapsed on the bed next to his sweat drenched partner.

STRIPPING ASJIAH

Yawning, Danielle stretched and rolled over on her stomach. "That was only round one."

"So what you plan on holding me hostage in this room all weekend?"

"You got somewhere else you'd like to be?"

Looking at her butter pecan skin, he playfully smacked her on the butt before responding, "Maybe."

"And where is that?"

His hand gently rode along the arch in her back as he admired her backside.

"Right...here."

Giggling at what he was implying she sat up. "N'uh uh."

"C'mon babe, I promise to be gentle."

Danielle turned on the lamp and grabbed her clothes off the chair.

"There is nothing gentle about fucking me in the ass." Her voice became inaudible as she pulled her hoodie over her head. "Let me do you and you can tell me how it feels."

"Oh you got jokes Danny?"

"It's not a joke, it's a suggestion."She did an off balance hop-skip over to the dresser while pulling up her sweatpants.

"Like I said, let me do you and you can do me. Titt," Cupping her breast she swung her hip to the side and placed her other hand on her butt, for tat."

"That shit ain't gonna happen." Mike propped a pillow behind his head and began flicking through the free movie channels provided by the hotel.

"Yeah, I thought so. It's all fun & games until someone wants to poke you in the ass." Laughter spilt into the hallway as she opened the door. "I'll be back," Grabbing the ice bucket she disappeared.

BY SA'RESE

The corridor was dim giving the hotel an eerie feeling as the storm threatened to shut the power off.

Turning the corner she was momentarily knocked off balance as her face slammed into his chest.

"Fuck! Watch where..."

His shirt was ripped and he had blood all over his clothes. He smelt of alcohol and what looked like mucus and some kind of white powder had formed this disgusting looking crust underneath his nose.

He was huge. At least 220 pounds and it was all muscle. His presence frightened her, how did he get in here? Where was he coming from?

A low buzzing noise followed by more thunder and then everything went black. The lights flickered on and off and each time they came back on he appeared to be closer and closer to her.

Looking down he had the sudden urge to grab her by the throat and throw her into the room he had just come out of. He was sure she wouldn't put up much of a fight but he had to hurry up and leave before someone called the police.

He had been holed up in that room for too long, the maids were becoming suspicious. Curious about the man who never wanted room service, who always called down to extend his stay by using his girlfriends credit card, a girlfriend no one ever seen.

He could only imagine how he looked. He pushed past her, causing her to stumble against the wall and then hurried off towards the exit.

The buzzing became louder and just as fast as they had gone off, the lights came back on. Danielle finished her prayer, crossed herself and slowly opened her eyes.

STRIPPING ASJIAH

Everything inside of her told her to run back to the room and tell Mike what happened but instead she found herself staring at this partially opened door trying to decide whether or not she should go in. She was certain this was where that guy had come from and if he looked like that; what did the other person look like that he had left behind?

What if someone was in there and they needed help? What if they were dead? Her heart beat a mile a minute and her stomach was doing summersaults. Taking a deep breath she pushed the door open; had she known what was behind it, she would've left it shut.

BY SA'RESE

Chapter Three

"We're going to give you IV sedation. You won't be completely under so you'll still be able to talk to us, and hear what's going on but overall the chances of you remembering what happened are unlikely."

I felt like I was in a morgue as I laid on the cold table. I guess this was, in a way, like an autopsy except I wasn't dead, not yet at least.

"The veins in your hand are much better; I'm just going to run the line through there."

I wasn't sure if she wanted me to agree with her, so instead I turned my head and looked up at the overhead light as I waited for the anesthesia to take over my blood stream.

"Count backwards from ten and when you wake up it will all be over."

She made it sound like a bad dream. Like all I needed to do was shut my eyes real tight, be still, and that would make the boogeyman disappear.

Wrong.

I would wake up, go back downstairs and Freddy Krueger would still be there reminding me that some nightmares are for real.

I began my numerical decent into hell as the sound of the vacuum drowned out my cries. I wanted to get up, to snatch this needle out of my hand and leave this wretched place but I couldn't. I had promised him that I would go through with this. Sold my soul to the devil the minute I signed my name on the clipboard when we walked in.

I thought I could stall him, thought that if he saw what this was doing to me emotionally; he wouldn't push me so hard. I thought that maybe he would look at me and see that perhaps I would be a good mother; he would finally "see me", acknowledge that I was carrying his child and maybe change his mind.

I gave him too much credit, held him at too high of a standard. I thought he would consider what I had already been through, everything that I had lost already, think about what this would do to me mentally, but he didn't.

It was obvious that he didn't care. How can you say you love someone and in the same sentence ask them to have an abortion? How was that love? And if that was love, what had I been feeling this entire time that we were together?

He gave reasons to a certain degree. Told me that we were too young, we weren't ready and we didn't need a baby right now. If that was the case I could easily say that we were too young to be having sex. Anytime you lay down with someone, protection or not, you're taking the risk of conceiving a child.

I was too young for a lot of things; I wasn't ready for a lot of shit. I had to grow up a lot faster than I would've liked, I was thrown into life's ocean and it was either sink or swim. I chose to swim. Looking back, it would've been so much easier to drown, to just let go and allow myself to be swallowed by the tide, allow the salty water to invade my lungs and flood my memories with sound.

But none of that mattered now.

Instead, I would let the surgeon drain my uterus, reach in and dismember my child like they were taking a car apart. I would drift off into a drug induced bliss and awake ignorant to the fact I had just murdered my baby. All of this because I believed in "happily ever after", I believed in his words, I believed that one day he would keep his promise, ask me to have his child and everything would be "perfect", just not now.

Right now my eyes are heavy and the lights are becoming faint. A single tear escapes my eye as I mourn for not only my child, but myself because not only was I killing an innocent fetus, I was committing suicide as well.

STRIPPING ASJIAH

Chapter Four

She wanted to scream as she looked at the image before her. The monster in front of her couldn't be real. As she stared into the mirror she was horrified at her reflection. She had prayed for her eyesight and now she wished that she had remained in darkness.

Her eyes were slits underneath flesh that was discolored. Her right eye was blood shot red, she was sure a vessel had burst. Lips that used to form a perfect pout now looked like she had gone twelve rounds with Mike Tyson. Her entire body was covered in bruises. There wasn't a part of her that wasn't black, blue, purple, or green.

The worst part was from her waist down. Her pussy was three times its normal size and she could now see that when she thought she had peed on herself earlier it was actually blood. She was bleeding; not only from her vagina, but from her anus to.

"What the fuck happened to me?"

Her voice was hoarse as words escaped her lips. She began to shake uncontrollably as she stared at the blood that covered her hands.

The power went out again and for a moment she saw him; he was punching her in the face, telling her that she wanted him, that he loved her and that she should shut up and take it.

She remembered fading in and out of consciousness. Blowing kisses at death, reaching out to touch it, unable to die because he would find a way to bring her back, back to him, to this room.

BY SA'RESE

She remembered trying to fight him off but the coke had her in another mind state, it had crippled her senses, blurred her ability to distinguish between fantasy and reality and as much as she wished she was dreaming, as much as she wanted to believe this wasn't real; the ugly truth was staring her right in the face.

Someone was entering the room. Straining her ears she listened for footsteps. Her heart felt like it was in her throat. The bathroom door creaked open as she managed to hide behind the shower curtain just in time. She held her breath praying that he wouldn't hear her. She knew if he found her, he would definitely kill her. A big part of her wished he had finished the job the first time around. Why not put her out of her misery instead of leaving her half dead to wallow in it? What else did she have to go through before God would allow her the sweet comfort of death?

Before she could question her fate any further her answers were revealed as the stranger spoke.

"Hello?" Tip toeing, Danielle looked around. "*What the hell happened in here?*"

The sheets were no longer white; but a dark crimson. Clothes were thrown across the floor, and the table and chairs were turned upside down. There was blood spattered across the head board, and on the vodka bottle that sat on the nightstand.

The storm began to resonate startling her as lightening shot through the sky. She walked towards the bathroom cautious not to make too much noise as she searched the rest of the room.

"Is anyone in here?" Danielle wasn't sure what she expected to find but she wasn't ready for what emerged. She looked on in terror as a female's hand pushed the shower curtain back.

"Ho dios mio."

STRIPPING ASJIAH

Danielle caught the girl just as she was collapsing. She couldn't be any older than herself. What happened to her? Who would do this to another human being? She shuddered as the image of the man in the hallway flashed back into her mind. It was obvious that it was her blood that stained his t-shirt.

"Please...please help me."

Tears flooded her eyes as she thought about the pain she must've endured, all the horrible things she went through as he assaulted her. How long had she been here?

There were bite marks on her fingers, her cheeks; some of her hair had been pulled out. Her ribs were discolored and her abdomen was swollen, signs that she could possibly be bleeding internally. Her jaw appeared to be broken and her shoulder looked dislocated. How was she still alive?

"Don't worry; I'm going to call an ambulance." Danielle looked down at her life like corpse and hoped she had enough left in her to make it to the hospital.

"Can you tell me your name?"

This is it. She had been granted this little bit of strength only so she could look herself in the face and see what her choices had led up to; self destruction.

She could feel her life slowly slipping away. Her eyes were too heavy and it was getting harder and harder for her to breathe. She mustered up everything that she had and tried to tell her who she was. She couldn't die without her knowing her name. The police would need to know so they could notify her mom when it was time to identify the body.

Wheezing she tried to speak.

"Key..."

"Take your time, I know it hurts." Danielle tried to support the girls head so she wouldn't choke on her own blood.

BY SA'RESE

"Key…Keyshia."

"Okay Keyshia, everything is going to be alright," Fumbling with the phone, she called the cops.

"I need an ambulance at 24 Public Square room 315; please hurry!" Danielle gently rocked the dying girl back and forth, praying softly as they waited for help to arrive.

"Dirty bitch, that's what she gets for thinking she could just walk out on me. No one leaves me."

Amidst the shadows of a dark alley Cash watched as the ambulance carried her away. It didn't have to end like this. Things were going so good at first; she had her head buried in his lap licking coke off his dick. Then when everything was gone, she wanted to leave. She laughed at him, insulted his manhood and thought she could just walk away.

He recognized the Latina girl from the hallway as he watched her talk to the paramedic. "I should've killed her when I had the chance."

He hadn't planned for things to get that messy, but the little bitch kept screaming.

It wasn't like he was doing anything wrong; he could tell that she had been run through a few times given the way he easily slid into her pussy. If she would've cooperated she would've enjoyed it; maybe showed him a thing or two; instead she wanted to yell and cry like a baby so he had to silence her.

He smiled as he remembered shoving his fist deep into her vagina. She pretended as if she didn't like it but he could tell by the way she was moaning that she fucking loved it, every minute of it.

STRIPPING ASJIAH

She stopped crying once he got in that ass though. How sweet it felt to open her tight little asshole until she lost control of her bodily functions and defecated on him.

On nights when his body failed him, he jammed the vodka bottle inside of her and fucked her with the cold, alcohol filled glass.

"Nasty whore; she was nothing like my baby." He felt an erection come on as he undid his jeans and began to stroke himself at the thought of her, "My sweet baby."

As her face began to take form in his mind he ejaculated all over the bum that was sleeping at his feet.

"You've been a very bad girl Asjiah; and when I find you Uncle Cash is going to have to teach you a lesson."

Chapter Five

I had been accepted to Clark Atlanta University and would be living in a single room in Bumstead Hall. My way out had come in the form of grants and scholarships that would allow me to leave this black hole of a city otherwise known as Cleveland.

I was packed and ready for my winged chariot to take me away to soul food and sweet tea in sunny Atlanta, Georgia where I would lose myself on Peachtree Street. Or so I thought.

I believed that I could start over and meet some sexy boy from one of the schools that made up the AUC and that wearing his varsity jacket would erase all the ill shit that had happened to me in that house but I was wrong.

I hoped the southern accents of the Atlanta natives would drown out the boring Midwest drawl I was used to, and that the word "shawty" would replace all the "blue eyed bitches" I had been called. I thought I had calculated everything perfectly, but somehow I managed to leave out the one thing in the equation that was now causing me to subtract everything that had added up to this moment; CJ.

My dreams of going to school had passed two months ago, the minute I found out I was pregnant. How was I supposed to walk on the cheerleading squad and expect to be a flier when I was carrying a baby? This was definitely not part of the plan. I felt as though he set me up. I mean sure, I had laid down and had sex with him but if I recall, I asked him to put on a condom. No, I didn't protest when he said he didn't have one and that's my mistake, one that I now had to suffer the consequences for.

Instead of unpacking and arranging my new dorm room, I was waiting for my name to be called so the baby mechanics could come lube me up, rotate my tires, and replace my engine.

"Asjiah Cappelli?"

A middle aged white woman who resembled Mary Poppins appeared in the lobby.

I didn't want to get up. Maybe if I just sat here for a while she'd go away.

CJ's eyes locked with mine and for a moment I thought he would say something, tell me that he didn't want to do this, that being here was a mistake. I thought he would take me away from this awful place but he didn't. I took my ring off and placed it on the table in front of him. His pathetic ass couldn't even look at me.

"Asjiah Cappelli?" Repeating my name she glanced over the chart as she waited in the doorway.

"Is there an Asjiah Cappelli here?" Mary Poppins' voice grew sterner as she glanced over the girls in the waiting room.

"That's me," I didn't recognize my voice as I spoke. I sounded like a frightened child. In a sense, I guess that's what I was. I got up, rolled my eyes at CJ, and then walked towards the door.

"Right this way Ms. Cappelli."

Ms. Poppins smiled at me as I followed behind her and scenes from the movie began to play through my head. In the film, her character was this perky nanny who could fly by using her umbrella. Looking at her I knew there would be no sing a' longs and that there was no way a spoon full of sugar was going to make this medicine go down.

"Hello?"

BY SA'RESE

"What's up shorty?"

"Don't what's up shorty me nigga, did she do it yet?" Corey rummaged through her closet as she tried to find something to wear.

"Man chill out, we at the clinic now; they just called her name." CJ looked around paranoid that the nurses were listening to his conversation.

"I can't believe you were so careless. You told me that you weren't fucking her raw CJ; you told me you and that little white bitch was over." Looking in the mirror, she held up a black jumpsuit; frowned, then put it back in the closet.

"I've been patient long enough Christian, I'm not going to keep warming the bench while you play house with her."

"Listen, I told you it's being taken care of. Soon enough it will be me and you again."

CJ put his head down and ran his hand across his head. The week him and Asjiah spent in Miami was perfect, just like old times. To see her smile again made him happy, how was he supposed to tell her that he didn't want to be with her anymore, that once they got back to Cleveland it was over? She had been through so much already and he didn't want to break her heart.

The image of her standing in front of the bathroom wearing the teddy she had bought from Victoria Secret almost made him second guess what he was doing. She looked so pretty. She was finally ready to give herself to him under the belief that he was hers and hers only.

"I'm sorry A'."

"What?" Corey took the phone away from her ear and looked at it. "What did you just say?"

"Huh?"

"You just said I'm sorry A'."

STRIPPING ASJIAH

Shit. He was losing it. Asjiah didn't deserve this but it was too late to turn back now. Besides, she wanted that nigga Money anyway. He wasn't sure when they had gotten so close but he didn't like it. Money always seemed to be there when he wasn't. Not only that, but Angel was cool with him which made him look even better in Asjiah's eyes.

"I don't have time for this shit right now Corey; A' is upstairs bout to kill my seed and you're whining; you're so fucking inconsiderate."

"Incon..."

Before she could finish, the phone went dead in her ear.

How did I end up here?

I was still in shock that CJ even uttered the words abortion. I didn't expect him to be ecstatic about my pregnancy but I thought he would get over it in time and come to accept it. Hell, I didn't know how I was going to take care of a baby neither but I knew I was going to try. I had already lost too much, too many people; I wasn't going to allow my child to be another one.

The door opened interrupting my thoughts and Mary Poppins entered; she was the psychologist? Great, I have to deal with her again.

She sat behind the desk, pushed her glasses up to her nose and cleared her throat before speaking.

"Ajeeiah."

"It's Asjiah. Like the country." Minus ten; she was already off to a bad start.

"Oh, I'm sorry. Well Asjiah; my name is Dr. Phillips and I wanted to ask you some questions before we go any further with the process.

"*Process*, you call killing an unborn child a process?" I could feel the baby shift to my right side. I placed my hand against it in an effort to calm things down.

"Now, now young lady; there is no need to get upset. I just need to know if this is really what you want to do. I know a lot of times girls get bullied into these situations because the person they are with, or their family, thinks it maybe the right thing to do; but it isn't about them. It's your body; therefore it's your decision."

She was right. It was my decision yet I had allowed CJ to convince me that *we* didn't need a child right now, that *we* weren't ready for the responsibility. What about what *I* thought?

"So is this what you want to do?" Ms. Poppins stared back at me with her hands folded and waited for me to respond.

My first reaction was to say; bitch does it look like this is what I want to do? But I couldn't; I knew I should've said no. I knew it was wrong. The baby gently kicked my side as a signal to tell me to speak up but I couldn't. I was scared.

I knew Marie would have a field day with this if I came home with a child. Would she put me out once she found out I was pregnant? What would I do then? I had already lied and told her that my housing had been screwed up so I had to sit out a semester. What would she say if she found out the real reason I wasn't going to school was because I was pregnant?

"Asjiah?"

"Yes."

"Yes; is that your answer?"

Tears began to pour down my cheeks and my heart felt like it was in my throat. What had I just agreed to? I had just signed my child's death certificate. I placed my hand to my swollen belly and instead of kicking; there wasn't any movement at all. I'm sure it was aware of what was about to happen.

BY SA'RESE

Chapter Six

CJ watched her as she slept peacefully in the backseat. She had this thing she did with her lips, it looked as if she was pouting or waiting for someone to kiss her. She looked so angelic, so peaceful. Amidst all the chaos that was surrounding her, he was glad that he could finally take her away.

Girls like Asjiah were rare. Smart, ambitious, sexy, caring, loving, but street at the same time. With everything he had put her through she still stood by his side. Loyalty was a trait not many people had but once Asjiah pledged hers to you; she was down for you no matter what.

He just needed her to wait, that's what the ring was for; to symbolize a promise that once he was ready, he would come back to her. Sure it was selfish to ask her to sit on the backburner until he got his shit together but he couldn't allow someone else to wife her.

He made the mistake of cheating with Corey; he never really broke things off with her, she was his side chic; the only setback with that is he knew Asjiah wouldn't play second to anybody, especially Corey.

He had feelings for both of them, but the problem was they were enemies. Corey and Asjiah hated each other yet he loved them both for different reasons.

He practically grew up with Corey. At first she was like one of the boys; she would play ball with them, watch sports; to him she was just little snot nosed Corrine from around the corner. But as time passed she traded in her baggy jeans for a pair that showcased these new found hips she had developed and her once flat chest now boasted d-cup breasts.

After playing hide-n-go get it; they had their first kiss and a few days later she allowed him to put his thirteen year old penis inside of her.

Corey had always been his safety net; she was there to catch him every time he fell whether it was stealing money from her parents to bail him out of jail, letting him stash his drugs at her mom's crib, or being his alibi when he needed one. She was his ride or die chic and he thought no one would come in between them until he met her.

It was easy to fall for Asjiah because she didn't have to try and be anything or anyone but herself. She didn't care what other people thought of her and he admired that. Her personality was contagious and she made it easy for him to be himself around her. She wasn't moved by the money he spent on her, the gifts he bought; all she wanted was him.

She was a good girl, his sweetheart; she kept him focused, grounded, she offered a distraction from the normalcy of life. She inspired him to do something better, to want more for himself, she was his better half.

Staring at her he realized just how much he had taken her for granted.

"Wake up baby girl."

He watched her as she stretched, rubbed her eyes and put on her sunglasses.

"Welcome to the Royal Palm's at South Beach."

"We're staying here?"

He helped her out the car and smiled as she adjusted her ponytail and tried to knock the wrinkles out of her orange linen Enyce dress.

BY SA'RESE

"What's wrong you don't like it?"

"Like it? CJ I love it!"

"Excuse me sir, would you like some water while you wait? We have tea and coffee as well."

"What?" CJ sat up in the chair and looked around. For a moment, he had forgotten where he was until he noticed all the pregnant girls around him. He had drifted off for a second, allowed his mind to replay memories that he tried so hard to forget; needed to forget in order to move on.

"No thank you."

"Alright, let me know if you need anything." The nurse slid the glass window closed and returned to her paperwork.

CJ quickly picked up the diamond ring that lay neglected on the table in front of him and put it in his pocket.

"Alright, I need you to roll up your right sleeve and relax. I'm going to draw some blood; this will only take a few minutes."

I stared blankly at the nurse as she tapped gently on my arm. She probably had a daughter my age; I could only imagine what she thought of me.

"See, all done. The doctor will be in shortly to escort you to the ultrasound room." She collected the sample she had taken, labeled it, and left the room.

I wanted to throw up; I was literally making myself sick. I was a coward, a punk; I had something to say any other time but when it mattered the most, when someone's life depended on it; my child's life, I couldn't say shit; pitiful.

"Hi. Asjiah?"

I looked up to see another doctor standing in the doorway. It seemed like everyone wanted a piece of the action. Everyone wanted to partake in the death of my child. I felt like they were all trying to dismember me piece by piece.

"I need you to follow me; we're going to do a quick ultrasound just to make sure there aren't any complications before we move on with the next part of the procedure."

There was that word again; Poppins had said process, now she was saying procedure, they all made it sound like I was here having a routine pap smear. Didn't they have the least bit of sympathy for what I was going through?

Then again, in their line of work I guess you had to be a little callus. I mean, how many times had they done the same thing to a million other girls? I was no different than the fifteen year old that was sitting next to me in the lobby. To them I was just another fast ass girl that had managed to get myself knocked up fresh out of high school.

"Okay, undress from the waist down and then we'll start the exam."

I felt like a puppet. Like Geppetto was above me pulling the strings making me do all of this. It was like I had been sedated but the anesthesia hadn't kicked all the way in so I was still conscious; still aware and being forced to go through the motions.

"This gel is going to be a little cold; I promise it won't take long." She pressed a few buttons on a machine and like magic my uterus appeared on the screen.

At first it was a little muffled but then I heard it; loud and steady like a bass drum underwater; one-two, one-two, one-two.

The entire time I had been lying on the table with this cold ass jelly on my stomach I didn't look at the screen. I didn't want to see anything that resembled another life form. But then this foreign voice escaped my lips and suddenly I was asking to know the sex of the baby. I wished that I could somehow reach out and take my words back but it was too late.

Why was I torturing myself? How would knowing the gender of my baby help me?

I turned my head and faced the doctor not sure if I really wanted her to tell me but a part of me felt like I should know who I was killing. All murderers identified their victims at one point or another.

"Unfortunately, you're only eleven weeks so it's too early to tell. Usually around twenty weeks if the baby is in a good position, we can tell you then."

In a thirty-second time frame I felt so many different emotions. I was disappointed because I would never know what I was having, I felt relieved because not knowing was preventing me from attaching myself any further than I already had, and I felt upset because I was putting myself through all of this.

I wanted to tell her to wipe the gel off my stomach, to pull my shirt back down and let me out of this room but I couldn't. I was silent.

I felt brainwashed, all I could hear was CJ's voice, it was like I was under hypnosis and my agenda was to do one thing and one thing only; terminate.

CJ reached into his pocket for his cell which had begun to vibrate. Looking at the caller ID he exhaled and answered the phone.

"What?"

"What do you mean what?" Corey's voice dripped with annoyance. "I've called you like three times now, why didn't you answer the phone?"

"Just like I said; what do you want Corrine?"

"Well, is it over? How much longer do I have to wait? You said you were coming to get me after you dropped her off; it's almost noon. I'm hungry CJ."

"Go get something to eat then," As he listened to her complain he was beginning to think that he had made the wrong decision.

"What I want you can't buy at the store." Corey laid back on her bed and crossed her feet in the air.

"And what is that?" CJ adjusted his jeans and smiled as he listened to her seduce him.

"You; I need you to come take care of me."

"I'll be over there as soon as I'm done here."

"Hurry up," Corey massaged her clit as she thought of him being inside her. "I don't know if I can wait much longer."

"Don't start without me baby,"

"Ah..."

"Uh uh; tell me you'll wait for me."

Annoyed, she licked her finger, got up from the bed and decided to take a shower to cool herself off until he arrived.

"Fine,"

Hanging up the phone CJ glanced at his watch. Corey was right, how long was this shit going to take?

This was the last step.

As I reached the top of the staircase I could see little areas sectioned off by curtains, giving privacy to the recovering girls that had gone before me.

"Right this way."

I felt like I was floating as I followed the nurse towards a medicine cart.

BY SA'RESE

"Here, take these then wait in the room down the hall. You'll begin to have severe cramping but they're just contractions. Someone will come in to check on you and make sure you've dilated enough and then you'll be escorted into the operating room."

She left me alone in the hallway with this Dixie cup filled with pills; one red, one blue. Funny, I didn't feel like Alice in Wonderland. For a minute I zoned out and found myself waiting for a bunny in a waist coat to come and tell me that I was late and show me the way out of here but it never happened.

I knew that neither one of these pills would shrink me and allow me to walk out of here unnoticed nor would the other make me a giant and allow me to step on CJ's throat for putting me through this shit.

I knew the minute I swallowed them I would seal my child's fate. The little heart that I heard beating just a few minutes ago would stop. The little hands that I saw would now wave good bye.

I found a bathroom down the hall and splashed water on my face. I flicked some of the water off my fingertips onto the mirror and watched as the drops created streaks distorting my reflection.

"What the fuck am I doing?"

I placed my hands on each side of the basin, closed my eyes and tried to clear my head. This was my baby, a life that I helped create, someone who was depending on me for survival and here I was contemplating ending its life.

I began to think that all the doctors and the nurses that I had talked to today were all angels trying to guide me and push me to make the right choice. All of them except for the bitch who handed me this cup; she had to be the devil; waiting to claim my baby.

I felt a kick as tears rolled down my cheeks. Too many times I had allowed the actions of others to dictate my life, I was tired of doing as I was told, tired of going with the flow just to get by.

My life had been disrupted because of one man's decision and that one single act had triggered a snowball effect.

My mother would never be by my bedside as I delivered my first kid; she wouldn't be present at my wedding. There were so many aspects of my life that she wouldn't be a part of. My father would never walk me down the aisle, he wouldn't get to meet my boyfriend, and they would never get to do the "traditional" before you marry my daughter type thing.

So many things that others took for granted, I had to think about because the dynamics of having a relationship with me were completely different than that of an average girl.

If I chose not to have this abortion, things between me and CJ would never be the same. We wouldn't be able to come and go as we pleased without having to find a babysitter first, things would be placed on fast forward and all the pressures and stress we never dealt with before would be staring us right in the face.

There were a lot of things I had yet to experience in life, but was that enough to validate my reason for doing this? Could I be that selfish? Could I allow myself to be swallowed up in the avalanche?

"Fuck this."

I walked over to one of the stalls and tossed the pills into the toilet. Pushing the lever, I smiled as swirls of red and blue mixed in with the water and then disappeared.

I found myself whistling Supercalifragilisticexpialidocious as I walked out of the bathroom and went back downstairs.

BY SA'RESE

Chapter Seven

"Hello?"

"You have a collect call from: LT.*"*

"Press one to hear the charges for this call, five to accept, or simply hang up to deny."

She had been avoiding him for the past three weeks in hopes that he would get the hint but it seemed like the more she ignored him, the more he called her.

She carefully placed the pregnancy test on the counter, washed her hands, took a deep breath then pressed the corresponding key.

Beep.

"Bitch you don't know how to answer the muthafuckin' phone now? How many times do I have to call yo'ass?"

Stacey's heart skipped as she listened to him yell obscenities into the phone.

"Fuck you."

"Aw Stacey, don't act like that baby; I'll take care of that as soon as I get out of here; maybe you'll let me in the back door this time."

"What happened between us was a mistake and you know it."

"Do I? I mean, to me it seemed like you liked it."

"I was only pretending to enjoy it so you could hurry up, bust and get the fuck off me." Stacey tapped the counter impatiently as she waited for the colors to appear.

"Deny it all you want girlie but I know what it really is. Don't worry, it's our little secret."

STRIPPING ASJIAH

"Not for long because I'm going to tell Angel what happened and then…"

"And then what?" Brushing off her threat he tried to contain his laughter. "What you think this nigga is gonna forgive you and welcome you back with open arms?

You must've forgot who the fuck we are talking about. The minute you tell Angel I had your legs spread across your kitchen counter, you're as good as dead to him. You might as well start planning the memorial now."

"Fuck you." She could feel her face begin to get hot as her temper flared. "You better hope I'm not pregnant or you're going to be laying in a box right next to me!"

"PREGNANT?" Startling the other inmates behind him; LT put his hand around the receiver in an attempt to muffle his voice.

"Oh what's wrong? You don't sound like you're holding your nuts anymore." Gaining control of the conversation she continued to taunt him.

"Wait until Angel finds out that you raped me *and* got me pregnant."

"What the fuck did you just say? Bitch I didn't rape you! You're talking real fucking reckless right now. You wanted me to have it. You were into that shit, throwing your hot ass coochie at me like some little bitch in heat."

"It's my word against yours and who do you think Angel is going to believe after you tried to have him robbed and killed? Tsk, tsk tsk…" Stacey twirled the phone cord around her fingers and smiled, "Now who's the bitch?"

"This call will disconnect in thirty seconds."

Afraid of what would happen if Angel actually did believe the lies she was telling; LT began to try and calm her down.

BY SA'RESE

"Listen, why don't you come up here and see me so we can talk; I'm sure we can come to some kind of agreement."

Stacey didn't have to think about it; without Angel around she didn't have anyone to take care of her. She was running out of the little bit of money she had stashed away and she wasn't trying to get a regular job.

Maybe she could get Angel to come off some money too; she was sure if he believed she was pregnant he would do anything for her. He was responsible for her becoming accustomed to this lifestyle in the first place so he should have to pay for her to maintain it. LT's petty cash would be an added incentive. His sex game was on point, but it was of no use to her now so his money would have to do.

"You have five seconds."

Stacey took a sigh of relief as she looked down at the minus sign.

"Goodbye LT."

"Stacey!" Punching the wall his knuckles split on impact. "Stacey!"

"Your chic got you that mad man?" A tall, brown skinned boy stood behind him snickering as he watched his hand begin to swell.

"Mind your fucking business." Without looking up, he brushed past the curly head stranger and stormed off to his cell.

"Hey-" Holding his hands up in surrender the boy stepped to the side and let him pass. "It's not that serious my dude; it's just pussy."

Had LT been paying attention he would've seen that death was staring him right in the face.

A smirk spread across Gabriel's lips as he watched him disappear across the pod, "Wait until I tell Angel this shit."

BY SA'RESE

Chapter Eight

It seemed like the storm had intensified as lightening ripped through the sky and the rain continued to flood the streets. Sirens blared as the ambulance came to a screeching halt in front of the ER.

"What do we got?" The female attendant rushed to the side of the gurney as the paramedics lifted the girl out of the wagon.

"Hypertensive with massive blood loss, respiratory rate is eight; she's still alive but I can barely palpate her pulse."

"Is she going to make it?" Danielle tried to speak in between sobs as she questioned the EMT.

"This young lady was with her when we arrived."

"Is she going to be okay?"

More nurses and residents ran to the side of the stretcher as they tried to assess the situation.

"BP's 70 palp, respiratory is eight and shallow, pulse is 130 after two liters of NS. Set up a central line; we need blood."

Suddenly all eyes were on Danielle as the nurse turned towards her. "What's her blood type?"

"I...I don't know." Confused and covered in blood she tried to get her thoughts together.

"Does she have any allergies, is she on any medications?" Another doctor chimed in as they tried to get more information about the young girl.

"I...I'm not sure. I don't know her, I found her in a hotel room."

"Is there *anything* you can tell us Miss?"

Feeling helpless Danielle began to cry as she shook her head. "No."

"Alright, we need an OR people let's go!"

Leaving Danielle in the waiting room, the doctors rushed off in a desperate attempt to save Keyshia's life.

"Beep…Beep…Beep…Beep.

Other than the constant red light that imitated her heart beat Keyshia was surrounded by darkness. The doctor's voices were faint as pieces of her memory started to materialize in her mind.

"Did I say you could leave? You thought you were going to come in here, smoke all my shit and bounce without giving me some pussy?"

Gasping for air Keyshia clawed at his hands trying to release his grip on her neck.

"Now strip bitch!"

She didn't like the look in his eyes. They looked cold, vicious. She wasn't sure if he was playing or being for real. The coke had her doubting reality. Her heart began to race as he threw her towards the bed.

"Listen up; the plan is to control the bleeding, repair the organs if there's any damage and get out as fast as we can!" The surgeon shouted instructions to the rest of the staff as they prepared to operate.

She wanted to tell them to stop. That she wanted to die, that her life wasn't worth saving but she was quiet. She was a zombie, doped up and in no control of her body; just as she was when he raped her.

"I said strip!" Growing impatient he charged towards her striking her violently across the face splitting her lip.

BY SA'RESE

"Fuck you!" The drug raced through her body, created illusions in her brain, making her think that she could challenge him. Keyshia stood defiant as she wiped blood from her face. Her intoxicated mind struggled to think of a way out. With open palms she slapped his face harder and harder hoping it would make him stop.

"Pressure's sixty over forty; she's losing blood faster than I can transfuse it in!"

"What's wrong baby?" Aggressively he palmed her breast "You had all kinds of shit to say a little while ago, don't get quiet on me now."

Biting his forearm, stunning him momentarily; Keyshia rolled out of the bed and ran towards the door. She felt like she was floating and she knew that her addiction was going to be her down fall.

"She's in v-fib! Charge the paddles to two hundred!" The doctors tried to remain calm as they watched the girls body jerk in reaction to the shock that was sent through her chest.

Keyshia could feel her soul leaving her body. She always knew she would die one day but she never thought it would be like this.

"C...CJ."

My eyes watered and I felt nauseous as I thought of how close I had come to killing our child.

He barely heard me as he looked up from his phone. "Asjiah, baby; are you okay?"

CJ held me as I began to fall apart in his arms and weep softly.

"Shh...its okay babe, it's over; everything is going to be alright.

STRIPPING ASJIAH

"I couldn't do it."

"What?"

What once was a tight embrace now felt as if he was shoving me off of him as he placed his hands on my shoulders and held me at arms length.

"We can't have a child right now." His face was filled with discontent as his eyebrows furrowed displaying his frustration.

"I know, but I...I just couldn't."

He couldn't believe what he was hearing, after she took her ring off he knew for sure that she was going to go through with it; now she was standing here saying she had a change of heart?

"Asjiah we talked about this."

I thought he would kiss me, wipe my tears away and tell me that he didn't want me to do it. Tell me that he was seconds away from coming upstairs to get me and take me home but he seemed annoyed, bothered by the fact that I decided to keep the baby; our baby.

"No, *you* talked about it!" I pushed him away from me and snatched my purse off the chair next to him.

"This chop shop was all your idea. I never wanted to come here, you're the one that bitched up and got all scared when I told you that I was pregnant. You never asked what I wanted."

"Asjiah..."

Before he could finish, our argument was interrupted by the receptionist.

"Excuse me, but you two are going to have to take this elsewhere."

I looked at her and rolled my eyes. Mad that she so willingly took his money when we first arrived, mad that she looked at me as if I was just some loose booty ass girl that got pregnant. I was mad that I had even allowed him to bring me here in the first place.

"No problem, we were just leaving!" I swung the doors open almost hitting CJ in the face as I walked outside.

"Out of all people I would think that you would understand how I was feeling right now. This isn't some rabid dog that needs to be put down; we're talking about a baby; *our* baby." I zipped my sweatshirt and pulled the hood over my head as the wind blew and it began to drizzle.

"I tried, I really did. With each room they took me into, every doctor that came to talk to me; I kept telling them I was sure; that this is what I wanted until I realized that I was only doing what *you* wanted me to do. I was laying there being poked and prodded like some lab rat because this is what *you* thought was best. Fuck what I had to say huh?"

"Asjiah that's not true, I just want you to think about what you're doing. What are you going to do with a baby?"

"Listen to how you're talking to me Christian; what am *I* going to do with a baby? This is your child too or did you get amnesia at the same time you came in me?" I tapped impatiently on the roof of the Cutlass as I waited for him to open the door.

"Unlock this fucking door and take me home."

CJ's phone began to ring as he started the car; glancing down at the caller ID he immediately sent it to voicemail; Corey had been blowing his phone up nonstop, leaving messages of her masturbating, telling him what she was going to do once he got there; now was not the time to deal with her or her throbbing pussy.

"A', you know I love you…"

"You love me? Then what the fuck were we doing in there? If you really loved me, then you would try to calm me down, tell me that we can ride this out and that everything will be okay. You would be as convincing as you were the night we were in Miami and you told me to trust you. Instead you couldn't wait to get me here, every other day you were hounding me; did you call the doctor A'? When is your appointment A'?" I could feel my cheeks get hot as my temper started to get the best of me.

"That isn't love, that's inconvenience. Tell me something; did you ever really love me Christian? I mean be honest, or was this all just a scheme you put together just so you could fuck?"

CJ rubbed his hands together, looked at me and smirked, "Nah, not at all, but if I had known all it would take was a little fresh air and a view of the ocean; I would've taken you to Miami a long time ago."

Before I knew what happened I slapped him across the face. I stared at him daring him to hit me back.

"I told you about putting your hands on me Asjiah." His jaw clenched as his temper threatened to boil over.

"What's gonna happen CJ; you gonna hit me back? Pull this car over and post the fuck up then."

"You better chill the fuck out A'."

"Fuck you. You know what this year has been like for me, you know my story; everything that I've lost and you suggest an abortion like you're offering to buy me new shoes or some shit."

"I'm just trying to look out for you."

"Look out for me? Are you serious right now? Where the fuck was you at when I got raped? Where the fuck was you at when my brother had a gun to his head and I was running for my life?"

I clasped my hands together as if I was getting ready to clap for him as the answer to my questions came to me. "Oh, never mind; I forgot; you were fucking Corey."

BY SA'RESE

"I understand you're upset A' which is why I'm not paying attention to all the greasy shit you're saying right now but you need to calm down. I never said I didn't want a kid, I just don't think it needs to happen right now."

"Funny how you can say that when I clearly told you that I wasn't on anything; but I guess your nut couldn't wait; oh that needed to happen right then didn't it?"

"I don't know why you're making a big deal out of it when you're obviously fucking that nigga Money anyway, how do I know that it isn't his baby?"

"Money, I'm fucking Money?"

I don't know if I laughed because what he was saying made absolutely no sense or because he accused me of cheating to throw shade to all the dirt he had done.

CJ hadn't looked at me the entire time he was driving but as we sat on the corner of Lee and Harvard waiting for the light to change he turned to face me with eyes cold as ice.

"Yeah I heard about y'all kicking it when I was down in the Nati. It sure didn't take you long to start giving my shit away."

"You can't be serious right now. I've been around you all day every day since we found out I was pregnant; so unless I managed to figure out a way to magically remove my vagina and loan that shit out, I don't see when I could've possibly had the time or the opportunity to fuck him. Even if I did get it in with Money, you're not in any position to say shit about it, not after all the bullshit I found out about yo' ass."

Bear ran up to the gate and began to bark as we pulled into Marie's driveway.

"Asjiah...A' look at me. I'm sorry. We're both scared and we're saying a lot of hurtful things to each other. I didn't want you to have an abortion but I didn't know what else to do."

STRIPPING ASJIAH

"You could've stepped up, been a man about it and took care of yours." I continued to look out the window as he talked. "I didn't sign up for this shit CJ, let me out this fucking car."

"A', babe..." CJ gently placed his hand on my chin and turned my face. "I'm sorry, and if it's not too late, I want to be there; for you and *our* child."

I turned and looked in his eyes and for a second I believed him. I wanted to put this day behind us and move on. I didn't want to do this alone but how could I be sure that when things got hot he wouldn't try to walk away?

I felt his phone vibrate and before he could press ignore I snatched it away from him snickering as I looked at the caller ID.

"What the fuck do you want?"

"Bitch, put CJ on the phone, I didn't call to talk to you."

"Bitch? You real muthafuckin' bold when you're on the phone, you must've forgot I know where you live at."

"Whatever, bring yo' bright ass down here if you want to and you gonna get yo' ass beat white girl."

"Word, I'm on my way."

"Asjiah give me the phone."

My right eyebrow rose as I snapped my neck back and whipped my head in his direction. "Give you the phone? You actually want to talk to this bitch?"

"You heard em', give him the phone."

"Shut the fuck up Corey." I looked from the phone then to CJ as I had a moment of clarity, "Wait a minute...does she know?"

"Give me the phone Asjiah."

"Answer the fucking question CJ, does she know?"

BY SA'RESE

He couldn't look at me; instead his face displayed this blank, stupid ass expression. His silence gave me the answer I needed.

I didn't know what else to say, I flipped the phone shut and threw it in his face hitting him square in the nose before getting out the car.

"Take yo' phone. I should punch you in your fucking face!"

"Asjiah,"

I was crying more out of anger than sadness as I listened to him yell my name. I wasn't going to turn around but he needed to hurt as much as I did. I walked back up to the driver's side and stopped a few feet away from the window.

"What do you want?"

"A', it's not what you think. I stopped fucking with her a long time ago but she keeps calling."

I reached through the window and touched the side of his face, "Its okay baby, I believe you."

CJ stared back at me confused. "You do?"

"Yeah,"

"Good, because I don't wanna fight with you A', get back in the car; I'll take you to get something to eat and we can go back to my house."

"Nah, it's cool. I'm gonna call Money; I'm sure he knows how to be faithful, besides if this was his child, I think he would be happy to know that I'm having a boy."

CJ's throat suddenly felt dry.

"It's a boy?"

I didn't wait to see the reaction on his face instead I threw my hood back over my head as thunder signaled the oncoming storm.

STRIPPING ASJIAH

No I didn't know what I was having, and yes it was wrong of me to lie to him but why should I give a fuck about his feelings when he clearly didn't give two shits about mine?

"I'm having a son?"

Asjiah's words kept replaying over and over again in CJ's mind as he drove down 116th towards St. Clair.

He had been so adamant about her having an abortion, so insensitive to what she was going through to the point where he disconnected himself from her pregnancy entirely. But now things had changed, not only had she decided to keep the baby but she was carrying his son.

The sudden realization of this mornings events and what almost happened came rushing to him all at once as he opened the car door and threw up in Corey's driveway.

"What's wrong with you?"

"Nothing,"

Corey stood on the front porch and looked at CJ in disgust as he wiped vomit from his mouth.

"You really need to learn how to control that little bitch of yours."

"Not now Corey."

Her legs glistened underneath the last rays of sunlight as the sky turned dark and water poured down from the clouds.

"I missed you," A short, black satin robe struggled to contain her voluptuous body as she walked towards him in four-inch heels.

"Now that it's over, we can finally be together."

"It's not over."

"You're right baby, it's just the beginning." Corey squatted in front of CJ carefully balancing herself on her stilettos, "I never felt like we were over anyway."

BY SA'RESE

Usually just the thought of her lips on him got him off but it wasn't working this time. Instead he was thinking of Asjiah and how broken and afraid she looked when she told him she couldn't do it. He was thinking of how betrayed she must've felt when she took her ring off, how tears flooded her pretty blue eyes as she disappeared behind the doors with the doctor.

"Get up." CJ grabbed Corey by her wrists and pulled her off the floor.

"What's wrong?" Corey placed her hands on the side of his neck and tried to kiss him.

"Don't let her get to you."

This moment didn't feel right, having her lips pressed against his made him want to throw up again. How could he have chosen this over the mother of his child? He shouldn't be here; he needed to be with Asjiah.

"I think that's enough small talk; why don't we get to what you really came here for." Corey slowly pulled the tie that was holding her robe closed allowing the delicate satin to fall to the floor exposing her body as it shimmered from the baby oil that covered it.

His eyes took in the perfect melon shape of her breast, and traveled down her stomach to her freshly shaven mound.

"I can't do this." CJ walked past Corey and towards the front door.

"Put your clothes back on Corrine."

"What? You make me wait all day while you hold little Miss Perfects hand as they suck out your love child only to come over here and say you can't do it?"

With the door half way open, he paused, "*My* child, she was about to kill *my* child and I was going to let her."

STRIPPING ASJIAH

"What the fuck do you mean about to?" Suddenly irritated, Corey ran her hand through her head grabbing a handful of her hair.

"Had you been listening to what I was saying instead of trying to put my dick down your throat then you would've heard me the first time; she didn't do it. Asjiah kept the baby."

"She did what?"

Looking at Corey's nude body he regretted that he had allowed things to go this far. Was he that sprung over her that he would sacrifice the life of his child?

"I'm out yo'."

Stepping outside he turned around just in time to see her slip and fall on her robe. A slight grin spread across his lips as he walked towards his car leaving her alone, naked, in the middle of the floor.

"Turn her on her side; give me a 60cc syringe and a spinal needle."

Keyshia cried out in agony as he shoved his dick inside of her infected pussy. For hours he raped her over and over again.

"Pulse/ox is coming up."

A sigh of relief washed over the staff as they all exhaled.

Suddenly everything seemed as if it was on fast forward. The bright light that had beckoned for her to walk towards it slowly began to disappear.

Everything began to rush into Keyshia's mind at once and although she didn't know his name, she knew his face; his eyes, but most of all she remembered that horrific scar across his neck.

"Alright, good job everybody; now let's get her closed up."

"Excuse me." Tapping the sleeping girl lightly, the nurse waited for her to awake, "Miss?"

Danielle opened her eyes and sat up immediately once she recognized the nurse.

"Is she...?" Worry filled Danielle's deep brown eyes as she searched the RN's face for answers.

"No...no; it's okay. She's stable. She's being taken to the ICU for recovery."

"Can I see her?"

"She's heavily sedated due to her injuries, but sure; I'll take you to her." The nurse took Danielle by the hand and helped her up from her seat.

"I have an extra shirt in my locker that would probably fit you."

"Huh?" Danielle looked down and realized that she probably resembled something out of a Stephen King movie.

"If you need anything you can go to the front desk and have the receptionist page me; my name's Ashley. Your friend is down the hall; room 3a."

Her feet felt like cement blocks as she approached the room. All of her emotions began to spill over her cheeks as she looked through the window at Keyshia.

Bandages covered most of her swollen face, a sling was supporting her left shoulder and IV's were hooked up to her arm, one most likely giving her medication while the other supplied blood.

Chills caused the hair on the back of her neck to stand on end as she thought of the man she encountered in the hotel hallway. What if he would've grabbed her? Would he have killed her or just beat her and left her on death's doorstep? She could've easily shared the same fate and been lying in the room next to her. Why had God spared her?

She inhaled and exhaled deeply trying to calm herself. She didn't want to start crying and appear weak when it was Keyshia who was in the most pain.

She quietly pulled up a chair and sat down.

"Hey, I don't know if you can hear me but you're safe now."

Taking her hand, she wrapped her rosary around her fingers and began to hum softly until she fell asleep.

BY SA'RESE

Chapter Nine

"A-ja! A-ja!"

As soon as I entered the house, Hope was the first one off the couch to greet me.

She was sitting in the front room with the other kids watching 101 Dalmatians.

"A-ja the dogs say woof! Woof! Woof!"

Picking her up, I laughed as her cheeks turned a bright red, "Hey Mama."

"Hi Asjiah," The other foster kids; Tiffany, Dorian, and James all waved hello to me without taking their eyes off the screen.

"Hey everybody," I placed Hope back on the sofa and went into the kitchen.

"Well it's nice to see you still live here; where you been at?"

I really wasn't trying to do this with her right now. I had been through enough and it was barely after one. All I wanted to do was take a long hot bath, eat, and go to sleep, "Over CJ's house."

Marie looked over her glasses and gave her granddaughter a quick once over, "Oh yeah?"

Before she could grill me any further, I opened the door to the hallway and went upstairs.

Almost two months had passed since I had actually spent the night in my own room.

Marie didn't really protest or try to stop me from leaving. I think she found comfort in the fact that I would be going to school soon so she gave up on trying to tell me what to do.

Given everything that had happened over the summer there really wasn't shit she could tell me anyway. You couldn't protect me from your son, so did she really think I was going to listen or take her advice on anything else?

When I told CJ I was pregnant he insisted that I stay with him. At the time I thought it was a good idea due to everything that had happened to me here, little did I know he only wanted to keep me under constant surveillance to make sure I actually went to the clinic. Too bad his little plan didn't work out.

My room was always the coldest in the winter and the hottest in the summer; now that I was with child my body temperature made everything seem ten times worse than what it actually was.

I took a quick inventory of my closet and my bedroom making sure everything was how I left it the last time I was here. Satisfied I took my shoes off and gathered toiletries so I could bathe.

I liked my bath water hot. Almost to the point of scalding but comfortable enough so I could sit in it. In some weird way I thought that having the water this warm cleansed me of any impurities that the world had rubbed onto me during the day. I thought that it helped rid me of any bad thoughts I was having at the moment; that it created this steam inside my brain that covered my subconscious in fog and allowed me to think clearly.

I undressed and submerged myself into the searing tub of water blocking out everything else around me.

I traced the faint line that had begun to appear on my stomach and smiled as I thought of how much my life would change over the next seven months. I entertained baby names although I was unsure on whether I was having a boy or a girl but I was getting tired of referring to my child as "it".

"Baby Jai,"

BY SA'RESE

I liked the sound of that. Jai could be a boy or girls name and it provided comfort in the simple fact that it reminded me of my mother.

I lost myself in the scent of Dove body wash and daydreamed about all things baby until my fingertips and toes resembled shriveled grapes. I dried off, wrapped myself in a towel, put on my robe and went back upstairs to my room.

I had overlooked the neatly folded stationary when I first walked in here, reaching for the letter; I spread it out on the bed so I could read it while I moisturized.

Asjiah,

I wrote this letter a while ago as a precaution in case something happened to me and if you are reading this; then you already know what it means. Before you get all worked up, don't worry; I'm fine. I know you may not understand my reasons for doing certain things but know that your big brother is a lot smarter than you think he is.

A lot of shit went down over the past few months, we had people close to us take their masks off and reveal their true faces, some stabbed us in the back as soon as they got the chance to; shit I'm still trying to pull the knives out of mine. They're trying to break us A', tear us down until we have nothing left. I'm not going to let that happen.

I can't go into detail but know that everything can't be handled in the streets; sometimes you have to submerge yourself in the jungle in order to catch the lions, sometimes you need to be standing right in the middle of the grass in order to see the snakes feel me?

Gabe and I are locked up out in Mansfield; not to worry little baby, I haven't left you alone. Soon enough you will see who really has your back. In exactly two weeks I need you to come and see me; until then be safe.

STRIPPING ASJIAH

Love always,
Your guardian Angel

P.S I know how much you've wanted a car, look underneath your pillow and you will find the keys to a brand new Civic. It's in the back yard in the garage, hope you like it.

I felt dizzy and the room began to spin. I placed my hand on my stomach hoping my sudden change of emotions wouldn't provoke the baby to make me throw up. When the hell did all this happen? I looked down at Bear who was lying at the foot of my bed as if he could answer my question.

"Angel's in jail?"

BY SA'RESE

Chapter Ten

The full moon casts an eerie glow into an almost pitch black room. The steady ticking of the clock made it hard for him to fall asleep, not that he could go anyway; tonight his mind was filled with fantasies, thoughts of what it would be like, what it would feel like to hold him. He wasn't sure when he first began to have these feelings but it seemed as if they were getting stronger and stronger.

His little cousin Micah was at the age where he was beginning to inquire about girls and sex and he would always come to him with his questions. However it didn't seem like the boys curiosity was being fulfilled with words, to him it seemed like he wanted live demonstrations, experiences that would help him to better understand.

Micah looked at him the same way his sister looked at his father the first time he pleasured her. Sure, she would say that she didn't want it to happen but he had witnessed the whole thing and he knew she was lying, he saw the passion in her eyes, the uncertainty that came from not knowing what to say, not being able to relay the feelings that she had for him. She wanted it. Her mouth said no but her body said yes.

She always wanted to be the woman of the house, and acted as if she was while their mother was gone; his father had merely given her the opportunity. Showed her what it was like to be just that; a woman.

He laid in silence and listened to the sounds of the house. If these walls could talk all of his family's dark secrets would be told. They would tell stories of his mother's rape, the infidelity, the incest; to him his behavior was normal, he was simply another apple that had fallen off his father's tree.

His breathing was steady as he got up and walked over to where his cousin was sleeping. He was filled with this nervous energy, this uncontrollable desire to touch him. Careful not to wake him, he pulled the comforter back and got into the bed. Micah's fourteen year old body was so warm, his skin was so soft. Nestling his head behind his neck he inhaled the alluring scent of cocoa butter. His hands traveled down the front of his pants until he was holding his adolescent penis.

"What the...." Startled Micah tried to turn around.

"Ssh...it's okay." Covering his mouth with one of his hands he hushed the frightened boy's voice forcing his head back towards the wall while he pulled his pajama pants down with the other.

"No...no..." Barely audible Micah hoped someone would hear him.

"I promise, it's gonna feel real good."

Without warning he pushed himself inside of him causing Micah to yelp in pain. He could feel the warmth of his tears wash over his hand as the frightened little boy cried.

He knew they were tears of joy, tears of elation, of relief that finally he was getting what he wanted. He was doing nothing but giving Micah what he so eagerly asked for. Showing him how to be a man, how to let go of his insecurities and indulge in his sexual desires, he should thank him. Now he would know what to do with all the little girls he liked.

Pumping back and forth, he continued to sodomize the young boy until the sun came up.

BY SA'RESE

The knock on the door was faint, maybe if he wasn't so exhausted he would've heard it, he would've had time to run back over to his bed and pretend as if nothing had happened, but as he listened to the knob turn and the door squeak open he knew it was too late.

"Noooooo!"

Kim stood in shock as she looked at her son. At first she thought he was dead. His frail body was still and the sheet he was using to cover himself had spots of blood on it. Looking from him to her nephew she was confused, her mind couldn't process what had happened although all the details were right in front of her. Before she knew it her hands were around his neck and she was dragging him out of the bed.

"You sonofabitch, how could you do this?"

"He...asked...for...it..." Gasping for breath he tried to free himself.

"Kim!" Jai rushed in the room and immediately tried to help her brother.

"This sick bastard raped Micah! He raped my baby!" She began to cry again as she tightened her grip, "Look what he did to my baby!"

"Stop, let him go, you're gonna kill him!"

A passing car snapped Cash back into reality as the bright headlights threatened to reveal his hiding place. Stepping away from the blinding light, he camouflaged himself behind a tree.

Jai was so naïve, so blind to what was really going on; she didn't know any better, she was only trying to help. Staring at the window Cash watched as his niece's bedroom light came on.

"Had she known I would be the one to take her daughter's virginity she would've let Kim kill me."

Chapter Eleven

I wasn't able to sleep for long. After reading Angel's letter I drifted off for a moment only to awake with the fear that someone was watching me. I got up from the bed, and stared out into the night.

For a moment I was certain that I saw him, standing right across the street waiting, stalking, plotting out his revenge. Was I crazy? I mean I saw the blood myself, I slit his throat. I knelt in front of him after he collapsed on the floor; I was there staring into his eyes as his life faded away.

Angel shot him; there's no way he could've survived. It couldn't be.

Cash was dead right? Wasn't he?

I looked out my window one last time before checking the locks and closing the curtains. I walked into the other room and made sure I had locked that door as well. It was too quiet in here, reaching for the remote I turned my TV on just as my cell started to ring.

"Hello?"

"Is this Asjiah?"

Great, just what I needed. Now I had to deal with some chic playing on my phone. I sprawled out across my bed and rubbed my temples, preparing myself for an argument.

"Who is this?"

"You don't know me but…"

"Listen, if you're calling to tell me that you already fucked or that you are fucking CJ, congratulations; thanks for joining the club, your t-shirt will be in the mail."

"Actually…"

"What? You don't want a t-shirt?"

"No, I…I…"

"You what; do you want a button or a key chain instead? A member's only jacket maybe?"

There was a loud noise in her background followed by a baby crying. I didn't know if I could take her telling me she was already his baby mama.

"No…I was calling because…"

"Because what? Spit it out."

"Keyshia's in the hospital."

"What?" I sat up and moved the phone to my other ear. Did I hear her right?

"What did you say?"

"She's at Cleveland Clinic in the ICU; you were in her phone as her sister so I…"

I didn't let her finish. I dressed, grabbed my jacket, the keys to my car and ran down the stairs.

Could this day get any worse?

I hate the smell of hospitals. Death seemed to linger throughout the hallways, loitering alongside the beds of patients near their last breaths waiting to carry them off to their final resting place.

I didn't like the fact that my mother never made it to the hospital. Doctors were never given the opportunity to save her. By the time they arrived at the scene it was too late. All that expensive equipment, all the time spent at medical school, the days and nights spent trying to save lives, none of that meant shit. It was all useless.

STRIPPING ASJIAH

I wondered if they would've been able to save her; if they would've been able to close all the holes caused by the knife that punctured her body over and over and over again.

Maybe…maybe then I would've had the chance to bring her get well cards, balloons, and teddy bears instead of going to the cemetery to lay down flowers that would never grow or get watered. No matter how pretty they were, they would eventually end up withered and dead, just like my childhood.

Had she made it to the hospital I would still be able to hear her voice, to touch her, to tell her I love her. But he didn't give her a chance. He made sure she would die; outside, in the cold, alone.

Maybe if the person who saw her would've called the police instead of closing their curtains and ignoring her, they would've gotten to her in time. Whoever it was, they were lucky I didn't know them because I would've tracked them down myself and killed them for doing nothing, for allowing her to die.

How could someone be that heartless? I heard that she actually managed to crawl to someone's doorstep, why didn't anyone bother to help her?

The red emergency sign sent images through my mind of the blood that we saw the next morning as a friend of my parents took Angel and I outside to see where it happened. Thinking about it now I wonder what they were trying to accomplish by doing that. Showing us the spot where my mother lay dying, fighting for her life, staring up into the heavens, why would you want to engrave an image like that into a child's mind?

Funny how the Bible teaches us that we are all God's children; that He will always be there for us yet he had abandoned her.

BY SA'RESE

My eyes watered making them appear as if the ocean was about to overflow.

"Get it together," Mumbling to myself I killed the engine, got out the car and walked towards the hospital.

"Excuse me."

"Yes?"

"I'm looking for a Keyshia Livingston." I nervously tapped my nails on the counter as I waited for the nurse to look up her information. I hadn't seen nor talked to Keyshia since her episode with Mike. Word around the way was she had a habit; and that she would do just about anything, with anybody, to maintain it. I hoped it was all lies but her being in the hospital made me believe it wasn't too far from the truth.

"She's in the ICU, room 3a. I need you to sign in and clip this to your shirt before you go see her."

I scribbled my name on the clip board and took the visitors badge before sprinting down the hallway.

Beep…Beep…Beep.

Danielle sat balled up in a chair as she looked from the heart rate monitor and then back to Keyshia. Although she had changed her shirt and freshened up as much as the hospital restrooms allowed; she still felt dirty; tainted with trepidation that antibacterial soap or antiseptic hand wipes couldn't cleanse.

She was afraid to close her eyes, apprehensive to allow herself to fall asleep out of sheer horror that the man she had bumped into in the hotel would be standing over her when she awoke. She had seen his face; he had seen hers; what if he came back for her?

"How is she doing?"

STRIPPING ASJIAH

Startled, Danielle jumped and looked my way.

"Sorry, I didn't mean to scare you."

"You must be Asjiah." Danielle finger combed her hair and tried to make herself look presentable.

"And you are?"

"Danielle."

I took a step back and watched her as she stood up. She was around 5'6" with wavy auburn hair that was swept up into a messy ponytail and big brown eyes; eyes that had seen better days. She reminded me of a young Rosie Perez.

After giving her a quick once over I turned my attention back to Keyshia.

"So what happened to her?"

"I...I don't know. We were staying in the same hotel and..."

"So you know her?"

"No...I was there with my boyfriend and I left my room to get some ice. I bumped into this guy in the hall and he had blood all over his shirt."

"What guy? Do you remember what he looked like?"

"No."

Danielle didn't want to say too much, she wanted justice for Keyshia but at the same time she was worried about her own safety. If she gave away too many details then that might prompt a police investigation and she was sure whoever the man was would get wind of it and come after her for ratting him out.

"I didn't see him. The storm knocked the power out before I could get a good look at him."

She closed her eyes for a minute in an attempt to block out the pictures in her mind.

"He didn't shut the door to their room all the way so I went in. I thought someone might have been in there; I caught her just as she was falling out of the shower."

I walked over to the bed so I could get a better look at Keyshia. If I hadn't read the chart on the door, and the nurse wouldn't have told me what room she was in, I wouldn't have known it was her.

She was unrecognizable. Someone had beaten her face to a pulp. Gauze was underneath her swollen eyes, tape and one of those metal splints covered her nose which had clearly been broken and a sling supported her left arm. I lifted the blanket to find that her ribs were tightly bandaged as well.

"Shit." I touched her hand in hopes that she would know that I was there.

"Who would do this to her?" Danielle stood at the foot of the bed gently tucking the covers around Keyshia's feet.

"I don't know."

"She could barely tell me her name when I found her; she was terrified, her body was in shock."

"It's a good thing you got there when you did."

"I wish I could've gotten to her sooner." Danielle's voice trailed off as she looked down at Keyshia.

"Then what; you would be in the bed next to her? You shouldn't blame yourself, there's nothing you could've done." I patted the fragile girl on the back and handed her a box of tissues.

"What kind of bullshit did you get my daughter into this time?"

The sound of her voice made my ears hurt. It was like hearing someone's nails scratch a chalkboard. I turned around to find Ms. Livingston standing in the doorway.

Keyshia and her mother looked just alike; they had the same peanut butter complexion and hour glass shape except Ms. Livingston was a little taller and her hour glass was beginning to resemble a lumpy water bottle. Her good looks were fleeting memories, a plot to a story that would tell of her glory days.

In some ways I couldn't fault Keyshia for her behavior because ironically her mother taught her everything she knew. The motto in their house was "use what you got, to get what you want" and that's exactly what her mother did.

Ms. Livingston changed boyfriends like I changed panties and with each man that left, he would leave some type of expensive gift behind.

I don't remember her ever working. She had assigned bills for each dude; or as I liked to call them; her sponsors. One paid her mortgage, the other paid utilities, one took her shopping and another was responsible for keeping money in her Gucci wallet at all times. I know where you think this is going but her tricks never harmed Keyshia. If anything they bought her presents as well; porcelain baby dolls, clothes, jewelry, and anything else she asked for.

Still none of the material things amounted to the valuable life lessons that are imperative with raising a little girl. Instead of helping her with her homework and teaching her normal shit that a mother should educate their daughter's about like how to cross your legs if you're wearing a dress or skirt, or about menstruation; she allowed Keyshia to hide in the closet and watch as she gave some guy head.

She let her come to toy and lingerie parties instead of allowing her to be around normal girls at sleepovers. Instead of teaching her how to ride a bike, she bought her a dildo and taught her how to ride a dick. By the time Keyshia reached middle school she could've taught our sex education class better than the teacher we were assigned.

"Excuse me?" Was she seriously standing here accusing me of being responsible for Keyshia's condition?

"Every time some shit goes down and my daughter is involved, I know you aren't too far behind. So what was it this time Asjiah?" Ms. Livingston adjusted her gold bangles, crossed her arms and glared at me with hate in her eyes.

"I didn't have anything to do with this. This is the first time I've seen Keyshia in at least a month or so."

"Why don't I believe that?"

"I really don't give a shit what you believe, when is the last time *you* saw your daughter? Maybe if you wiped the cum out your eyes you could pay more attention to her."

"You know I never liked you."

"The feeling's mutual."

"You think you're so innocent. You always thought you were so much better than my Keyshia. I've seen the way you look down at her. Maybe you're just jealous, maybe your envy for what my daughter has finally got out of control and you set her up."

"Jealous? I'm jealous?" I smiled, giggling a little at her insinuations.

"You're right, I am jealous. You have to excuse me because I'm a little bitter since I don't get as much dick as Keyshia does." I scratched my head causing my hair to frizz up a little giving me a disoriented appearance.

"Maybe I'm a little on edge because I have yet to take it in the ass; I'm not sure. Then again, maybe I'm angry cause I didn't get the starring role in last summers blockbuster; 'Let's bang the Crackhead'. I should write all this down so I can remember to ask her if she can teach me how to be a hoe when she wakes up. Danielle, you gotta pen?"

"I...I..," Danielle looked back at me puzzled not knowing how to respond.

"Your daughter don't have shit but a worn out pussy, broken ribs, a couple of stitches and a mother who never gave a fuck about her. I'm not loose like that and I think I'll pass on the assault and battery. And Oh, I'm pretty sure I got it covered as far as dysfunctional family goes."

Ms. Livingston walked further into the room until she was standing directly in front of me. "Listen here you little bitch..."

I slapped her hooker red finger nail out of the way and looked dead in her eyes.

"No you listen, I've had a very, *very* long day and I was trying to be respectful but I don't have the energy for yo' bullshit. She called me, not you so she obviously doesn't want you here; so why don't you go back to the dick you crawled off of and get the fuck outta my face."

This day had taken too much out of me and my patience was beginning to run out. She looked as if she wanted to hit me and I was ready in case she did. I had had enough of just about everybody so if she wanted to fight; fuck it, let's do it.

"Is everything okay in here?" Ashley; the nurse from earlier tapped on the door commanding our attention.

Ms. Livingston glanced at Keyshia, then, back at me before responding. "Yeah everything is fine."

"Well visiting hours are over, I'm afraid everyone's going to have to leave and allow our patient to get some rest." She walked over to the IV bag and began checking Keyshia's fluids.

Ms. Livingston knelt down besides her and whispered in her ear, "I thought I taught you better than this." She kissed her on the cheek, zipped her leather jacket and disappeared into the hallway.

Danielle waited until the chime to the elevator sounded before she spoke.

"So that's Keyshia's mom huh?"

"Yeah that's her, in all her slut-tastic glory."

"Do we really have to leave?" Danielle watched as the nurse continued to check Keyshia's vitals.

"No, you two can stay. I could hear you arguing from down the hall and it seemed like things were getting pretty heated in here so I stepped in." Ashley looked at the monitor, wrote some things down on the chart then turned back to us.

"If you two need anything just let me know, there's some blankets in the closet if you get cold."

"Okay, thank you."

I was beginning to feel nauseous, I hadn't eaten since yesterday and aside from a few sips of water nothing had touched my stomach. I got up and barely made it to the bathroom as I began to cough up the lining of my intestines.

"Are you okay?"

I started to dry heave as my insides convulsed in an effort to regurgitate anything it could. I had to remember that I was no longer eating for just myself anymore.

"Yeah...I'm fine."

Danielle held my hair behind my head and rubbed my back. "Are you hungry? Would you like me to run and get you something?"

I lifted my head, wiped my mouth and leaned against the wall. "You look like you need some food too."

As if on cue her stomach began to growl. "Yeah I guess I do."

STRIPPING ASJIAH

"I could use some fresh air why don't we go to the Chicago Deli over on Euclid."

"Sounds good,"

"Where'd you park?" I grabbed my navy Polo jacket off the chair and waited for her to get her things.

"I didn't drive. I rode in the ambulance with Keyshia." The sliding doors opened, prompting her to rub her arms vigorously.

"Here." I handed her my jacket, zipped my sweatshirt and placed my hood over my head.

"Thanks."

"Don't worry about it."

"Sir have you been helped yet?" The nurse signed off on her charts and placed them in the appropriate bin before turning to face him, "Sir?"

"I'm looking for a girl; brown skin, maybe around 5'5". I think she was brought to this hospital earlier." His eyes darted nervously around the ER.

"Do you know her name?"

"Uh…," He was uneasy, jittery. He was taking a huge risk being out in public but he needed to know if she was still alive.

"Her name Sir,"

"Just tell me what room she's in."

"Due to patient safety, we can't let you any further than the lobby if you don't know her name."

"But I'm family."

The nurse was beginning to get suspicious; his presence made her nervous. "All the more reason you should know her name."

She managed to make eye contact with a passing security guard who seemed to sense her discomfort.

BY SA'RESE

"Is there a problem here Ash?"

He turned around to face the young man who was standing behind him with his chest poked out tapping on his gun.

"No problem at all," Glancing down at his badge he smirked. "Officer Bailey, I was just trying to see if my sister was here, but I guess she isn't." He winked at the nurse before stepping away from the desk.

"If you want I can look at that scar for you."

He had forgotten that his wound was exposed as he ran his hand across his throat.

"I'm good." Brushing by the officer he disappeared out the exit before she could say anything else.

"What was that about?"

"I don't know, he was asking about a girl that he thought had been admitted here but he couldn't give me any information on her."

"Yeah that's weird."

"Weird isn't the word, he was down right creepy."

We took our seats at the Chicago Deli and waited for the waitress to return as we looked over the menu.

"I'm sorry I was such a bitch to you earlier. This hasn't really been the best day for me." I placed my hands around the band of my sweatpants and rubbed my stomach.

"It's cool. Today hasn't really been my favorite day either." Danielle sipped her tea and began to relax a little as the peach flavored liquid warmed her body.

"Are you doing okay? I know that had to be really scary walking in on something like that."

"Yeah it was; I've never seen so much blood before."

STRIPPING ASJIAH

"It was that bad huh?" The apple juice I ordered seemed to sit well with baby Jai. Every time I would stop drinking it, I would get kicked.

"Bad is an understatement. It was gruesome. The sheets were bloody, the walls; it scares me just to think of what he must've done to her."

"I told her to be careful."

"What do you mean?"

"Keyshia is careless, too impulsive; she doesn't think things through."

"Cobb salad with ranch dressing," Danielle moved her hands so the waitress could sit her plate down, "And chicken tenders with a small fruit bowl." After asking if we needed anything else, the petite blonde girl smiled and walked away.

"So did you see anyone leave the room?"

My question made her fumble and drop her fork.

"No…"

"And you said you don't remember what the guy looked like that you ran into?"

Danielle hesitated before continuing. "I couldn't really see his face…"

Before I could drill her any further, her phone rang.

"Hey baby, what's up?"

I picked all the cherries out of the fruit bowl as I waited for her to finish her call.

"I'm fine, no; I'll be there later, I just wanted to make sure she was okay." Danielle held her finger up, suggesting she would only be a few more minutes. "Alright, love you too."

"Boyfriend?"

"Huh? Oh yeah, sorry about that. I left the hotel before I could tell him what happened, he just wanted to make sure I was straight."

I was getting ready to hammer her with questions about this guy of hers but before I could get my words together, she changed the subject.

"So what high school did you go to?"

"Keyshia and I went to South, you?

"Warrensville, is her mother always like that?"

"For the most part, but I only come around when she isn't there because as you can tell she despises me."

"It can't be that bad."

"Trust me, you don't know the half."

Danielle drizzled ranch dressing on her salad then continued.

"So how long have you two been friends?"

"Since elementary, she's like a sister to me."

"Then why haven't you seen her in a month?"

"What?" I pushed my plate to the side and sat back.

"You told her mother you hadn't seen her in a month or so. Why is that?"

"So now you're interrogating me too?"

"No...I was just..."

"You were just what?" I rubbed my scalp, cocked my head to the side and sighed.

"A lot of drama went down last summer, Keyshia got involved in some shit that I wasn't cool with and we stopped speaking. End of story."

"Sounds like, it's either your way, or no way."

"No, it sounds like you need to mind your fucking business." My leg began to twitch as I stared across the table at her. She was really beginning to irritate me.

STRIPPING ASJIAH

"Are you always this mean?"

"Are you always this nosy?"

"I'm just saying; it seems like you would be a little nicer to the person who saved your best friends life."

"So what do you want a cookie now?" I looked around the room for our waitress. "I can buy you a cookie if that would make you feel better."

"Fuck you." She tossed her napkin on the table and got up.

The other patrons in the restaurant turned and looked my way as Danielle stormed outside.

"Aww, did I upset you?" Laughing, I unlocked the doors to the Civic and allowed her to get into the car.

"Keyshia's mom was right, you are a bitch."

"No, a bitch would be telling you to give me my jacket back and putting you out of my car." I turned the key, and shifted the gear into drive.

"Listen, I don't know you, and you don't know me, but you seem like a smart girl so you should know that there's only so much advice you can give someone before you say fuck it and allow them to learn on their own. Keyshia thought she could fly so I allowed her to do so; now it seems like she's fallen flat on her face."

BY SA'RESE

Chapter Twelve

"One hundred forty-eight…one hundred forty-nine…"

"We need to talk." Leaning against the bars, Gabriel waited for him to finish his set.

"One fifty." Dusting his hands, Angel got up from the cold concrete. "What's up?"

"I got some news for you."

"News about what?"

"LT,"

"And, what about him?"

"Dog, I don't know if I should tell you." Gabe ran his hand through his already messy hair and pondered briefly over what he was about to say.

"Then what the fuck did you bring it up for?" The corners of Angel's mouth turned up as he twisted his lips.

Looking over his shoulder he made sure no one was listening before he continued. "I overheard him talking to Stacey on the phone."

"What?"

"Stacey nigga, I don't know what they were talking about before I walked over there but she must've told him she was pregnant cause right after he blurted that shit out, he punched the wall."

Gabriel watched as Angel put his fingers to his temples and slowly began to rotate them as if he was trying to massage the image of LT and Stacey out of his mind.

"You alright man?"

The look on his friends face made Gabe shutter. He was expecting him to start throwing things, or rush out of the cell, to go find LT and beat the shit out of him but instead he stretched out on his bunk and started laughing.

"First he tries to kill me and A', now he's gotten my girl pregnant? *This* nigga's ill." Angel became somewhat hysterical as Gabe stared at him puzzled.

"When I grow up, I wanna have balls the size of his."

"What you want me to do about it?" Gabe's adrenaline began to pump as he thought of all the ways he could make LT suffer.

"Nothing,"

"Nothing?"

Complacent, Angel sat up and suddenly the smile that had just danced across his smooth dark skin disappeared, "Nah, I got this one."

Chapter Thirteen

10/5/2000, 1:15am

Bullshit...

I can't sleep. I don't want to go to bed because I'm afraid the reel that is my brain will finally be put on pause and I'll be staring at a memory I don't want to relive.

I know it sounds crazy but I feel like someone is following me; someone meaning Cash.

I keep going over that day in my mind and there's no way he could've survived. Even if he was still breathing when I left him, there's no way Angel allowed him to live.

So if I know that, why do I still feel like he's out there?

My nightmares have gotten better but being in this house... walking past her room... up and down these stairs... it reminds me of how helpless I felt, how afraid and weak I was. Everyday I try to push it further and further back into my mind until eventually, hopefully, it'll just disappear.

Am I trying to ignore the fact that it happened?

No. I just choose not to deal with it. Why should I drive myself crazy trying to figure out reasons why this nigga raped me? Why should I sit around trying to understand why my uncle, my mother's brother, felt that it was okay to cum all over his nieces face?

I'm sure that dumb ass psychiatrist would tell me "let it out Asjiah, color your feelings" fuck that and fuck you too if you agree with that psycho babble bullshit.

STRIPPING ASJIAH

What is crying about it gonna do? It's not going to change the fact he went up in me raw now is it? Trust me, its better this way.

Bear has been sleeping in my room since I came back home. I knew if anyone came in here unannounced he would defend me. He was very protective of me and Angel, and in some ways I think he knew that my mother was gone. He was her dog after all.

Her…

I wish she was here. I miss her terribly, some days more than others. I definitely could've used her support today. I still can't believe I was about to abort my child. Where would I be if my mother would've chosen not to have me? What would my life have been like if I had been born to some other family? Would they have loved me more than the parents I have now?

Yes I know I said "have" and that's because I don't refer to my mother in the past tense. I refuse to acknowledge her death, that may sound crazy to you but I really don't give a fuck. Admitting she's gone means I would have to say goodbye and I'm not doing that.

It's been ten years since I've seen or spoken to my father and regardless of if I choose to ignore him for the rest of my life, the truth is, he's still alive.

If I had been raised by someone else, would my outcome be any different than what it is now? Would I have still been raped? Would Angel have still been beaten?

I can't answer any of those questions but if my circumstances were anything other than what they are, I wouldn't have known her and although we only spent eight years together, I wouldn't trade it for the world. Those were the best eight years of my life. I can only hope to be the mother she was and still is to me. I just wish we could experience my pregnancy together...

Marie didn't blink an eye when I came home. I didn't really give her the opportunity to question me but knowing her, I'm sure she would find a way to quiz me later. I thought she would've showed more concern, I mean hell, I've been gone for a minute but I suppose that's what I get for thinking because it was clear that she didn't care. A normal parent, guardian, or whatever the hell you want to call her, would've asked if I was okay, if I wanted to perhaps talk about the things that happened recently, but no, not her. Intimate discussions weren't her thing, compassion wasn't her forte and more importantly this entire set up was far from "normal".

CJ has left at least fifteen voicemails. I'm really not on him right now. You would think he would take the hint and just stop calling but he obviously isn't that smart. I can't believe he told that bitch Corey that I was pregnant. Was he calling her while we were at the clinic? I was about to murder our child and he was probably on the phone sweet talking that raggedy bitch.

If I wasn't pregnant I'd drive down to the Valley right now and fuck her up. Not because of CJ, nah, I'd beat her ass for disrespecting me. I mean, the bitch clearly lacks self respect; what kind of woman chases behind another nigga that has a baby on the way?

I guess I could pose the same question to his ass. What kind of 'man' was he to keep fucking around when we're about to have a child?

STRIPPING ASJIAH

More importantly, what kind of dumb ass was I to believe all his lies?

I thought they were done. After Miami I just knew that he had left her alone and that things between us were going back to normal. It couldn't have been any further from the truth. What was it about this girl that kept making him go back to her? Seriously, I mean did sparks shoot out her pussy when she came? Did she squirt platinum or piss diamonds? She had to be taking it up the ass, what else could it be?

She must've been calling him to see if I had gone through with the abortion. The nerve of this broad; and then he had the audacity to accuse me of fucking Money? Really?

Money...

I hadn't seen him since we had dinner at his house. Where was he? Was he okay? Wait a minute, why did it matter? He hadn't returned any of my phone calls or tried to call me so fuck him too. All that suave shit he was talking last summer about how he always had a thing for me, how he wanted me to be his girl, "I'ma take care of you A', if you were mines you wouldn't have to worry about shit A'...blah, blah, blah, yeah, yeah, yeah. He was on some bullshit just like Christian's ass.

Still, a part of me believed that when I really needed him, he would be there. As bad as it may sound, I was hoping that he would come and rescue me from the clinic; that all of a sudden I would hear his voice and everything would be okay. I was expecting him to appear like some knight in shining armor to whisk me away from the evil baby murderers.

Ha! I'm bugging out...

BY SA'RESE

Just when I was letting him get close to me he disappeared. Niggas. He could kick rocks right along with CJ.

It seemed like a lot of people had vanished since last summer and now they were all starting to reappear like ghosts or bandaged up mummies like Keyshia's ass. What the fuck had she done to land her in intensive care? It was obvious that she was still up to her old tricks and someone had caught her slipping or either wasn't falling for the okie-doke that she ran on these other lames and decided to beat her ass.

What threw me was her momma accusing me of being the reason why she was in there. Hell, for all I knew it could've been one of the many men she used to fuck with that finally decided to see if her daughter was a chip off the ol' block.

I sympathized with her in the manner that I didn't want to see her all stitched up like that and in so much pain but on the other hand I told her to slow down. You can't keep running red lights and expect not to get hit.

And who the hell was this Danielle chic? How much truth did her story hold? How did I know she wasn't involved? How did I know that wasn't her man that she bumped into in the hallway and that's the reason why she refused to identify him? It would all make sense if she was the scorned girlfriend and wanted to get back at her boyfriends bust down.

They both could've been part of the scheme. And what was up with him calling her while we were eating? What was he saying on the other end of the phone? What if he was calling just to see if Keyshia was alive, maybe Danielle was supposed to make sure she didn't live so she couldn't name them as suspects. She was too jumpy, too on edge and something about

STRIPPING ASJIAH

her didn't add up. I didn't trust her. It was going to take more than her calling the ambulance to get on my good side.

If there's anything I learned this past summer, it was to watch your friends closer than you did your enemies; your enemies may have the gun, but your friends are going to be the ones that hand them the bullets.

I closed my journal and stretched. After wrapping my hair and changing my clothes I decided to lay it down for the night. I placed my head phones on my stomach and set In a Sentimental Mood by Duke Ellington and John Coltrane on repeat.

I read somewhere that music was good for a child's development so I guess baby Jai was off to a good start. Besides, Love Jones was one of my favorite movies, a classic. I could have the next Darius Lovehall or Nina Mosley growing inside of me.

Chapter Fourteen

"Sign in, along with your name and the inmates CDC number. You can take up to $20.00 in singles, along with your car keys and I.D." The burly C.O watched as Stacey complied with her instructions.

"Make sure you empty your pockets. Everything needs to be in a clear plastic bag so that it's in plain view to the officers in the visitation room."

Stacey walked through the metal detector and into another small doorway as she waited for them to unlock the next door. Looking around she turned her nose up at the other females that were standing beside her. From the way they were dressed, most of them were probably coming to see their baby daddies, boyfriends, or like the big girl to her left; her pen pal.

Decked out in skin tight Akademiks jeans, a brown sweater and matching knee high boots it looked as if Stacey was coming to visit an incarcerated lover as well but LT was far from that. To her he was just a means to an end; the end being her money troubles. If she had to dress up and play the role just to get him to tell her where his stash was at; then so be it.

A loud buzz followed by a deafening clanging noise startled the women as they trotted through the door like cattle.

Beating the pack, Stacey was the first to cross over the threshold entering the visiting room.

"Sign your name and take a seat anywhere you'd like." Another manly looking woman barked orders at her from behind the desk.

After finding somewhere to sit, it wasn't long before she felt LT's hands on her shoulders.

"Shit, you look good as hell." Grinning from ear to ear he waited for her to stand up. "Can I get a hug?"

Although she didn't want to be anywhere near him she had to admit prison life had been kind to him. He was clean shaven and had a fresh line up. Whoever the fairy was that played prison barber was doing a very good job.

Stacey sighed softly to herself and extended her arms to welcome his embrace. She wasn't expecting the tingling sensation that went through her body causing her clit to pulsate as he hugged her tightly. She couldn't see through the plain, blue oxford shirt but she could feel the results of him hitting the bench as he held her.

Palming her ass, LT kissed her roughly on the lips before releasing her and pulling up a chair.

"I didn't think you were gonna come."

"I wasn't." Folding her arms, she tried not to make eye contact with him.

"C'mon girl, don't act like that. You can sit here and be all hard if you want to but you practically melted when I kissed you." Licking his lips, he smiled revealing deep dimples in both his cheeks.

Stacey shook her head and tried to get her mind right. "Why did you want to see me?"

"I needed you to tell me to my face if you were pregnant or not."

"I told you over the phone."

"So you should have no problem saying it again. Don't get shy now."

BY SA'RESE

Stacey thought for a minute before she spoke. She knew her answer would determine the outcome of how things played out. She knew LT had a thing for her since day one. Yeah, she had flirted with him too, but it was harmless fun. She never expected to fuck him, and it's not because she didn't want to, had he been some regular dude they would've got it in a long time ago but he was Angel's cousin.

He always seemed to be in competition with Angel and because of that he could very well take pleasure in the pain it would cause him to see his main chic walking around carrying another nigga's baby, his cousin's baby at that. But then he might ask for ultrasound pictures and she would have to find a way to make herself look as if she was gaining weight with each trimester.

She needed to step lightly. Proceed with caution. She just needed to milk him long enough to get her over until Angel came home.

But what if he decided to take his chances and he didn't care whether or not Angel knew? That was a risk she wasn't willing to take. If Angel found out, she was certain there would be a price on her head, if it came down to it, she would just lie and tell Angel that the baby was his. Stacey took a deep breath and decided to roll the dice.

"Well, are you carrying my seed or not?"

Playing with her hands she kept her head down long enough to make her eyes water before she looked up at him, "Yes."

LT was silent for a minute while he allowed her words to marinate.

"Shit." Wiping his forehead, he then cleared the beads of sweat that had formed around his nose.

STRIPPING ASJIAH

She tried to study his expression but he was blank. The cheery disposition he had when he initially said hi to her was gone. It seemed like hours passed between them before he finally spoke.

"How much does that shit cost?" Patting his pockets he acted as though he was going to hand her the money right there, "Four, five hundred dollars?"

"Fuck you."

Squeezing her thigh LT snickered, "That seems to be all you know how to do princess."

"I'm not getting an abortion."

"Oh but you are."

Realizing she would have to take this all the way Stacey mentally blew on the dice and rolled them again.

"It's too late for me to get an abortion. I'm too far along, no doctor will touch me."

"Then do that shit yourself." LT's eyes were dark as coal as he stared back at her emotionless.

"Do it myself? Are you fucking serious?" Stacey quickly put her coat on and got up, "I'll make sure to send Angel the ultrasound picture and let him know that it's yours."

"Sit yo' ass down." Grabbing her wrist he yanked her back into the plastic chair. "You ain't gonna do shit. Wanna know why?"

She snatched her arm away and turned her back to him.

"If you tell Angel what went down he's gonna put two and two together. Yeah, he may buy the whole I raped you bit for a second but then he's gonna realize that the only person who could've told me about his connect was you. And then what do you think your dark knight is gonna do?"

BY SA'RESE

Stacey's defeat began to settle in as her eyes started to create real tears.

"What's wrong baby girl?" LT's chair made a screeching noise as he slid it across the floor so that he was sitting directly in front of her.

"What, did you think I was gonna take care of you? Did you think I was gonna wife you once you told me you were pregnant? You didn't think I really liked you did you?"

"You weren't shit to me but a nut, a pretty piece of garbage that Angel dressed up in expensive, designer labels. I just wanted to see what that shit was hitting for, if it was as good as I thought it was."

Stacey sat in silence as she tried to think of something to say but the only thoughts she was having were those of shame and humiliation. She had driven all the way up here thinking that her pussy would prevail and that he would succumb to her needs but instead she had stepped in an arena where there was no room for little girls and childish games. This wasn't the sandbox and she was no longer in kindergarten trading kisses for Twinkies, the stakes were much higher and unfortunately for her, she had just crapped out.

The correctional facility looked more like a detention center or a reform school rather than a prison. I was expecting dudes with bowl cuts and matching uniforms to jog down the street chanting some rhyme that repeated the phrase "sound off".

I didn't know the details of Angel's sentence, but I did know my brother didn't belong here. Prison was supposed to house hard core criminals; pedophiles, rapists; niggas like Cash.

It was for embezzlers, arsonists, serial killers, murderers; people like my father.

STRIPPING ASJIAH

Angel was none of those things. Sure, he sold crack and I could see why some might frown upon his profession but he had a legitimate reason for doing so. You may not feel that way, but just in case you haven't been paying attention; I really don't give a shit.

I don't have time to debate everyone's opinion of my brother's lifestyle; because someone is always going to have one, and just like assholes, they're usually full of the same thing that comes out of them.

It's funny how older people can turn their noses down at us and point fingers but they were doing the same things when they were younger. That's all they did was have sex and get high, where do you think all of us came from? Hell, the majority, if not all of Angel's clients had been junkies since the seventies. He simply became part of a phenomenon that was going to continue to thrive with or without him.

Unfortunately along the way a few people died due to the treatment he provided to aid their addictions; but if it wasn't from the rock candy that they smoked or shot into their veins, it was going to be by some other vise of their choice.

You see, my brother never really had one of those; a choice that is, he wasn't given a fair chance; he had to hit the ground running and if that meant cooking up coke in order to put food in his mouth, so be it. He wasn't like these wanna be dope boys out here who did it for the attention, the money, or because they thought it was going to bring them pussy by the pound; Angel did it as a means to an end. He saw things on a grander scale, on a canvas so to speak; his plan was to paint a picture that would get him and I both out the hood.

Glancing in the rearview mirror I ruffled my curls and reapplied my Dior Reflect lip gloss and exited the car. Even though I wasn't showing, I didn't want to draw any extra attention to myself so I decided to wear black cargo pants and a white long sleeve thermal shirt that said BeBe down the right sleeve. I cinched the drawstrings just enough so they would sit perfectly around my black BCBG ankle booties.

I signaled the alarm on my car and walked across the gravel towards the entrance. Just as I was getting ready to go in; she came out.

"Stacey?"

I said her name more as a question to myself rather than a salutation.

"A'…Asjiah," Stumbling over her words she tried to force a smile.

"What are you doing here? Did you see my brother? Is something wrong with him?"

"Angel? He…"

Something about her wasn't all there. She looked as if she had just seen a ghost. Her eyes were red around the rims obvious proof that she had been crying.

"If something is wrong with my brother Stacey tell me."

"He's okay; it's just weird seeing him in here. The fact that I get to walk away and he has to go back to some tiny box bothers me."

She was avoiding eye contact, looking at the ground and acting as if she was in a hurry to get away from me. She was lying about something.

"Angel's been through a lot worse; its going to take more than jail to break him."

"Yeah, I guess you're right." Fumbling with her car keys she took a few steps towards the parking lot. "I gotta go A', it was nice seeing you."

STRIPPING ASJIAH

Stacey wanted to run to her car but she was sure Asjiah was still watching her. Her hands were shaking; she could barely put her key in the ignition. Her heart raced as Asjiah's words reverberated through her mind. *Angel was here?*

"Who you here to see baby girl," The brown skinned corrections officer smiled as he watched me approach the counter. The gold cap that covered his front tooth made the rest of his teeth look even more yellow as he tried his best to flirt with me.

"I don't think that's any of your business." I turned my nose up at him and reached for the pen to sign my name on the clipboard.

"Asjiah, that's a pretty name blue eyes."

His words made me think of Cash and I wanted to reach across the table and punch him in his fucking nose for calling me that, but if I did; they would cuff me in a heartbeat and throw my little ass in a cell for assault.

I didn't have time to come up with something witty to say because my attention was diverted elsewhere. Just as I was putting the pen back down I saw it; *Stacey Johnson.* And as my eyes followed along the line they read the person she had signed out; *Lashon Travis.* This bitch had been here to see LT!

My face felt like it was on fire as I counted softly to five in an effort to calm down. Why was she coming to see him? Did Angel know LT was here?

I didn't see my brother so I decided to get him a few things before the guards brought him out. There was no telling what kind of garbage they fed him in here. Although these canned juices, quarter bags of chips, and microwavable cheeseburgers

BY SA'RESE

weren't exactly gourmet dishes, it had to be better than the mystery meat he was eating.

"What's up pretty girl?"

"Really? I can't go to the fucking vending machine...," My voice fell short as our eyes met.

Dressed in Phat Farm jeans, a red long sleeved tee, and red, blue and white Timberlands; I had to do a double take to make sure it was him.

"Caleb!"

"What's good A'?" Caleb retrieved the apple juice from the dispenser and handed it to me.

"Where have you been? I haven't seen you in forever."

"I've been around, laying low, staying out the way." He rubbed his hands together allowing me to catch a glimpse of the platinum bracelet that peaked from underneath his sleeve.

I chose a section in the corner for us to sit. I knew Angel wouldn't want to have his back to anyone and this angle would give him a view of the whole room.

"You looking good."

"Thank you."

Sitting the snacks down on the table I tried not to blush as I felt my face become flush. Was Caleb flirting with me?

Before our conversation could go any further a familiar voice made me smile.

"Little baby,"

"Angel!" Jumping out of my seat I almost knocked him over as I hugged him. He had put on a little weight since the last time I saw him; of course I wouldn't admit to that because he would probably start flexing his muscles telling me how good he looked.

STRIPPING ASJIAH

Instead of the wrinkled, off brand blue khakis and button down shirts the other inmates were wearing, Angel's Dickies were neatly pressed and so was his shirt. As a replacement for the rundown sneakers they were given, a pair of fresh black Air Force One's were on his feet.

Noticing Gabriel behind him, who was just as clean as Angel, I rushed over and hugged him as well.

"What's up with you Caleb?" Angel and Gabe both took turns exchanging pleasantries with their friend.

"What's good fam?"

I felt like my family was being reunited as we all sat down and began to talk.

"So how you like your car A'?"

"I love it, thank you so much." It seemed as if all the excitement had awakened the baby. I ran my hand across my lower back as I felt Jai shift then reposition comfortably against my kidney.

"Your welcome princess; so how you been, everything okay?"

"I'm straight, how was your visit with Stacey?" I knew she had been here to see our cousin but I wanted to probe his mind first.

"What?" Angel's lip twisted in disgust at the sound of her name.

"Stacey, I just saw her outside."

Angel looked at Gabriel, who then looked at me before I continued. It was obvious that he wasn't aware of her visit.

"She was fronting telling me that she was all heart broke and shit about seeing you locked up in here and for a minute I actually believed her, until I signed in and saw her name next to LT's."

BY SA'RESE

Angel's jaw clenched tightly causing the veins in his temple to bulge. He thought she loved him, he had confided in her, told her things that he hadn't told anyone else and she had betrayed him. She wasn't deserving of all the things he had done for her. She was nothing more than a backstabbing, opportunist, selfish ass bitch.

Angel slouched down in his chair and pushed all thoughts of Stacey out of his head, he would find a way to deal with her later.

"So how long has she been fucking him?" I didn't know if he was really banging her but what other reason could she have for coming to see him?

"I don't know but Gabe overheard him talking to her on the phone." Angel took a deep breath, "She's pregnant."

"What?"

"Congratulations dude."

"Not by him dumb ass." I punched Caleb in his arm then turned back to my brother.

"Are you serious?"

Angel would never admit it, but I knew he was hurting, we all did. Stacey had somehow infiltrated the armor he had built around himself and he had given his heart to her.

"What about LT?" The wheels in Caleb's head were turning as he tried to piece everything together.

Gabe quickly picked up on Angel's mood and addressed Caleb instead. "He didn't notice me, so as of right now, he has no idea we're here."

"Shit, that's deep. How ya'll plan on handling that?"

"We…,"

Angel put his hand up to silence Gabe. "I haven't decided yet."

STRIPPING ASJIAH

The lack of emotion in his voice gave me goose bumps.

"And what about Stacey, do you want me to go see her?"

Angel smiled and tapped me on the head. "No, its cool Mighty Mouse, I'll take care of her."

"Are you sure? I can go over there as soon as I leave here." I wasn't in any condition to fight but I knew things would be one sided so I wasn't concerned with putting the baby at risk. I was simply going to knock on her door, and as soon as she answered, punch her right in the face.

"Yeah, it's cool."

His demeanor surprised me. I thought he would've been heated, irate at the fact his bottom bitch was sleeping with the enemy but he wasn't. He was chill, cool, and collected which only meant bad things for Stacey and LT.

"You quit fucking with that weak ass nigga CJ yet?" Gabriel leaned back in his chair and grinned at me playfully.

Sucking my teeth I looked back at him. For a brief second my phone call with Corey replayed and I revisited the anguish I felt in the abortion clinic.

"Actually I have."

"For real," Shocked at my response, they all replied in unison.

I raised one eyebrow, shook my head a little bit and twisted my lips giving them the 'duh' face.

"Yes for real."

"I told you that nigga was a lame." Angel's voice had an 'I told you so' tone to it as if he knew this was going to happen. He must've seen the hurt in my eyes because he quickly changed the subject.

"A', would you tell this nigga Gabe about the lil' airplane game we had when we were younger." Opening the juice, Angel took a sip from the perspiring can before placing it back on the table.

"Here he go with this shit." Gabe ran his hand through his hair causing his curly afro to appear as if he had just gotten out of bed.

"What airplane game?"

"You remember the one joint we had with the VHS tape; you had a red jet and I had a black one."

"Wait a minute," I put my head down and tried to recall the name of the game. "Captain Power!" Laughing I felt like a little girl again as I shouted out the name of one of our child hood toys. It was good to talk about our past; it let me know he thought of those days just as much as I did.

"I think ya'll be making shit up." Chiming in Caleb interrupted our celebration.

"That's what I said." Gabe dapped him up in agreement.

"Why we ain't never heard of no Captain Planet game?"

"Captain Power." I nudged Caleb in the shoulder teasing him for getting the name wrong, "Captain Planet is a cartoon."

"Whatever."

"Ya'll just mad cause we had all the rich kid toys and ya'll had all the bootleg shit." Angel clutched his stomach as he began laughing.

Caleb tapped my leg, "Yeah Ok, but now ya'll stuck up asses got the same shit we do."

We continued to reminisce and poke fun at each other before the conversation turned serious.

"We only got like a hour or so left on this visit so I think we should get down to business." Angel pulled his chair in a little closer prompting us to do the same.

STRIPPING ASJIAH

"As you know, we're probably going to do three years behind this bullshit and I can't afford to lose any money; hell, none of us can so I need someone to keep things running for me, someone I can trust." Angel looked from me to Caleb before continuing.

"A', I know you had your heart set on going to ATL for school but I need you here. It shouldn't be too late for you to enroll at Cleveland State; let me know how much your tuition is and I'll take care of it."

"I don't want to go to Cleveland State." I wasn't sure where this little discussion was headed but I didn't like it already.

Angel had always been protective of me and I appreciated that, but now he was trying to dictate where I was going to school? I wasn't on that shit. I've been trying to get out of Cleveland since I got here and now he wanted me to stay for another four years? Fuck that.

"I know you don't but let me finish. I need you to learn the campus. Make a couple of white friends, go to their parties and peep things out; they're going to be your customers."

"Customers?"

"Hold up, are you letting her run shit?" Caleb had been quiet the entire time but whatever Angel was talking about had obviously made him upset.

"Are you questioning me?" Angel's forehead wrinkled as he stared back at Caleb daring him to say something.

"Chill out; chill out." Gabriel placed his hand on Angel's shoulder and pushed him back into his chair.

"Nah, if he feels a certain way about it then he should have the opportunity to get it off his chest."

Caleb glared back at Angel with a look of disdain in his eyes. His knuckles were beginning to turn red as he gripped the side of the chair.

"I've been down with you since day one and this is how you repay me?"

"And how would you like for me to repay you; what do you want, some kind of ribbon for all your years of service nigga? What you want, a purple heart or some shit?"

Gabe could sense the tension that was growing between his friends and judging from my brother's temper and Caleb's mouth; he knew it was only a matter of seconds before one of them would start throwing punches.

"Both of you need to calm down. Caleb, I know you feel you should be next in line but regardless of how long we've been down with Angel, A' is his sister and he's going to choose her over us every time. Look at everything that went down with that corny ass nigga LT last summer, would you trust anyone after that?"

The irritation that cloaked Caleb's face soon subsided as he took in what Gabriel was saying.

"Um...," I raised my hand as if I was in a classroom and patiently waited to be called on. "I have a question."

"Yes A'?"

"I guess I'm a little slow today because I don't know what's going on. You're talking about me enrolling in State, partying with the white kids and them being my customers. What do I need customers for?"

"You know sometimes you are so smart and other times you are so fucking stupid."

Gabriel chuckled at Angel's comment.

STRIPPING ASJIAH

"Whatever Angel, just tell me what the hell you're talking about and quit acting like you're the fucking Godfather."

"I want you to take over while I'm in here."

Was he serious? I mean, I had run a few errands for him here and there, bagged a few things up and made a couple drops but now he wanted me to take over?

"Me?"

"Yes you A', no one would ever suspect it. When word gets out that I'm in here, nigga's are gonna expect for shit to be shut down and these happy ass little wanna be thugs are gonna try n' run wild. But if they still think I'm out there, then the balance isn't shaken up and shit still remains as is."

"But I…"

Angel patted me on my head and smiled. "Don't worry; I'm going to teach you everything I know. And Caleb will be there to make sure things run smoothly; right Caleb?" Angel stared into his eyes waiting for them to show any sign of disloyalty.

"Right," Caleb felt like he was going to choke as he swallowed his pride. He knew Angel hadn't made this choice to spite him and that his decision had come after looking at things from every possible angle.

Angel was always twelve steps ahead of everybody and he was right, no one would suspect Asjiah. Angel had given him a task far more important, he trusted him to look after something that didn't have monetary value, something that couldn't be replaced; his sister.

"Alright, visiting time is over!"

I turned around to find the C.O. that was aimlessly trying to game me earlier shouting from behind the tiny desk.

"Come back next weekend and I'll explain everything to you then. Caleb; I'll be in touch soon."

BY SA'RESE

Angel and Gabe said their goodbyes to Caleb and then hugged me.

"I love you little baby."

"I love you too Angel."

After watching them disappear behind the metal doors I turned and walked towards the exit.

"So you're Cappelli's girl huh?" The guard looked me up and down and licked his lips as I approached the desk.

I tossed my hair over my shoulder and smiled, "And what if I am?"

"Then I would tell you there's nothing he can do for you in here," Reaching across the table, he caressed my hand. "And that you should let me take care of you."

"Oh should I? And how would you do that?"

"I'd start by eating that pretty pussy of yours."

"Really, you know everything you put in your mouth isn't good for you."

"Let me be the judge of that."

I was trying so hard not to laugh in his face; I could tell by the way he was squirming in his seat that I was giving him an erection. This dude was too thirsty.

"And if he found out, what do you think would happen to that tongue of yours?"

"I ain't scared of that nigga," The C.O. sat up in his chair as if he was trying to somehow demonstrate his courage through good posture.

I leaned in a little further so that my lips were almost touching his earlobe.

"My guess is, he'd probably cut it out especially since I'm not his girl."

"You not?"

STRIPPING ASJIAH

"Nah, baby, I'm something much worse."

"And what could that be blue eyes?"

I jerked my hand from underneath his clammy fingers and grabbed my ID, "His sister."

BY SA'RESE

Chapter Fifteen

His eyes had become accustomed to the darkness. He knew his way in and out of her room with no problems. The closer he got it seemed like her scent grew stronger and stronger. He could navigate his way to her bedroom and back without bumping into anything. It seemed like an eternity since the last time he had been in this house, since he had felt her, since he laid unconscious on his mother's bedroom floor.

The thought of her lips around his dick had him anticipating each move she made, each touch, he closed his eyes and waited for his fantasies to come true but he would never get that sensation. Instead, he would open his eyes and find her kneeling beside him watching as his life faded away.

Rummaging through her dresser drawers he stopped once his fingers led him to what he had been looking for. He felt his dick harden as he held the soft cotton close to his face and inhaled deeply. The saliva from his tongue moistened the fabric as he licked over the crotch area imagining her labia in front of him. He placed the ones he had soiled back in the drawer and picked up a fresh pair of boy shorts; smelling them again before placing them in his pocket.

How long would he have to wait to be near her, to be inside her again? He wanted her to look at him the same way she did the first time; maybe she would finally tell him she loved him, that she needed him.

But these things took time, careful planning; he didn't want to scare her although he knew it wasn't fear that overcame her but an unspeakable feeling of desire in her eyes as she stared at him while he aggressively undressed her. He knew she wasn't fighting him; instead she was being playful, teasing him, and making him want her even more.

Why couldn't she understand that he never wanted to hurt her? All he wanted was to give her what she had been asking for all these years, he only wanted to be her teacher, and to him, she would be his student.

He wanted to give her pleasure, bliss, satisfaction. He wanted her to experience the same ecstasy he had given to Micah. She should be grateful. He had taken her virginity, opened her up, and with each stroke shown her how much she meant to him.

He thought she had finally stopped denying that she wanted him when he walked in the house and seen her in her underclothes. He thought that she would finally let go of her inhibitions, realize that they weren't doing anything wrong and just let things happen, to just allow love to take over, but he was wrong. She tricked him, played games with his heart and she needed to be punished.

Thoughts of that day began to flood his mind as he laid down in her bed. Would she be receptive if she saw him now? Would she try to apologize and make up for her wrong doings?

He would make her pay for her betrayal; she needed to feel everything he felt except this pain would be a lot different. He wanted her to enjoy it, to be conscious so she could watch everything he did to her. Most would call it torture, but to him it was going to be foreplay.

He tried to have a little fun with the last girl but all she wanted to do was get high. Did she really think he was going to allow her to leave him? She was too full of herself, too used to getting what she wanted and he had to knock her off her high horse. Her pussy wasn't as good as his nieces, it wasn't as tight, but he wanted her, in that moment she needed to be Asjiah.

He could tell she liked it rough; she kept trying to run away; kicking and screaming, slapping him, scratching his face. He could be aggressive too so that's the way he gave it to her. She spit on him, he spit on her; she hit him and he hit her back; except his punches drew blood and after the first couple of blows she didn't want to play anymore, she didn't seem like she was enjoying herself.

He had kept her in that room for two months, as long as he was a paying customer, the guest service attendants didn't bother him. To them he appeared regular, he spoke every time he walked through the lobby after leaving the hotel to get food, and the noises they heard could easily be ignored with the "do not disturb" hangtag they gave you for the door.

Eventually the money he had taken from her purse ran out, her credit card reached its limit, and he was getting tired of trying to keep her conscious so he left. He wanted to be with someone he loved, someone like Asjiah.

The up and down motion was creating a heat between his hand and his dick that reminded him of her warmth. He kept a steady pace as he thought of the smoothness of her skin, the firmness of her breast, the softness of her lips, and the pink rose in between her thighs that seemed to excrete honey as he plunged deep inside of her.

His hands suddenly became sticky as his thoughts erupted and he came all over her sheets.

"Hello?"

"..."

"Hell-lo?"

STRIPPING ASJIAH

"…"

"Bitch are you gonna say something or just listen to me breathe?"

"A', Asjiah it's me."

My stomach started to cramp as soon as I heard his voice.

"What do you want CJ?"

"I just wanna talk I haven't heard from you."

"Um, maybe that's because I haven't called you."

Ignoring her sarcasm CJ took a deep breath and tried to remain calm. "How are you and the baby?"

"Oh, now you're concerned? You weren't too concerned when you were talking to Corey while we were at the clinic."

"I didn't call to fight with you A'."

"You shouldn't have called at all." Pulling into the driveway I let out a sigh of relief noticing Marie's car wasn't here.

"I guess I deserve that."

"You deserve a lot of shit but I'm tired, I'm hungry, and I just got back from Mansfield so I really don't have the energy to play with you right now."

"You went to see Angel?"

"How did you know my brother was in jail?"

"C'mon A', when a nigga like Angel gets knocked, word spreads like wildfire."

"Well you can douse the flames and tell whoever is running their mouth that he is doing just fine."

"How did you get there?"

"What the fuck is this twenty questions?" Taking the rubber band from around my wrist I wrapped my hair in a ponytail.

"I drove CJ, that's how I got there."

"When did you get a car?"

"Why does it matter? Did you buy it? Is there a reason for all of these questions or did you just call me to get on my nerves?"

He wanted to tell her that he loved her; that he was scared, nervous about being a father but he couldn't. She was still upset and he knew until she calmed down there would be no reasoning with her.

"I just wanted to see how you were doing."

"I'm okay but I'll be much better when you get off my phone."

"Aiight A', you win." Feeling defeated he put his head on the steering wheel. He had no one to blame for the way things were between them but himself, at a loss for words he quietly held the phone.

"Hello?"

"Yeah, I'm here."

"Well say something shit." Swinging my bag over my shoulder I put my key in the door.

"I'm sorry A'."

"Eh...," Imitating a buzzer on a game show I turned the lock, "Times up. Call back when you have something to say that I can actually believe.

The clatter that the security door made caused him to jump up from the comfort of her bed. Panicking he scampered around the room as he tried to map out his escape. He couldn't go downstairs, what if someone saw him? What if it was her? As bad as he wanted to see her, now wasn't the time, he wasn't ready. He had to think, and fast. He silently cursed himself for being so sloppy, so careless. But then he smiled.

Looking at the bed he realized that she would see it, see the mess he had made on her sheets and she would remember.

STRIPPING ASJIAH

"I'm sorry A'." Mumbling I repeated CJ's words as I entered the house and locked the door behind me.

"Yeah I'm sorry too, sorry for believing all your bullshit."

Unlatching the door to the basement I waited until I heard the familiar sound of his paws against the cement. I smiled as the huge Rottweiler appeared at the bottom of the stairs.

"Hey Bear."

His nub of a tail wagged playfully as he waited for me to give him permission to move.

"Come on boy, come on." Backing up I moved to the side to give his mammoth sized body room to maneuver on the small landing. Squatting down I brought my face close to his and scratched behind his ears. I tried to spend as much time with him as I could because I knew he missed my mother as well.

We had gotten Bear off a puppy farm in Germany when I was around two years old. Angel and I wanted the runt out of the group; a tiny, energetic fur ball named Tarzan. But when my mom seen Bear it was over; he walked up to her, licked her cheek and she gave my father the 'I want this one face'. My dad, unable to tell her no, bought him for her and he's been a part of the family ever since; at least what's left of it.

He followed me into the kitchen where I placed my bag on the table and half heartedly began to search through the cabinets for something to eat. Of course there was nothing in the house that appealed to my cravings so I decided I would lay down for a minute then go up to Hot Sauce Williams.

Bear emitted a low growl as his ears twitched, then perked up.

"You heard that too?" I looked at him waiting to see if the noise would repeat itself but all I could hear was my own shallow breathing.

Silence.

And then there it was again.

Footsteps.

Above me.

In my room?

I cautiously walked to the hallway that led upstairs. I tried to steady my heartbeat as I placed my hand on the handle. Bear began to snarl showing perfect fangs; teeth that I knew would rip whoever was up there to shreds. I closed my eyes, inhaled deeply... exhaled slowly...and opened the door.

STRIPPING ASJIAH

Chapter Sixteen

Stacey paced back and forth in her bedroom occasionally glancing back at the money on her bed. Her plan to scam LT had gone to shit and she barely had a little over two thousand dollars. What was she going to do when it was gone?

She had been careless, stupid, and naïve to think that Angel would always be around to take care of her. She couldn't go to him and ask for help now.

Everything would start to unravel once Asjiah told him she had seen her. But what if she didn't? Wait a minute, what did she mean 'if'? She was positive that Asjiah had blurted out their encounter the second she saw Angel. It was only a matter of time before someone pulled the thread and the seams that were holding her together began to unravel.

She hadn't spoken to Angel since he got locked up. Given his reputation she was sure that he would be going to a fed prison. What were the fucking chances that he would get sent to the same place as LT? How was she supposed to know that? Did LT know? Did he allow her to walk into some big elaborate scheme that they had been plotting this entire time?

Her brain was in overdrive, she was becoming paranoid. She had been caged up in her room since she came back from Mansfield. How long could she hide here? She wasn't safe in her own house. She knew that if Angel wanted to get to her, no matter where she was, he would find her.

She nervously twisted a strand of the 2b Yaky through her fingers as she pondered her next move. Maybe she should just be honest and tell him what happened. Maybe he would forgive her, or maybe she could try to get Asjiah on her side and have her talk to him instead.

"Yeah fucking right," There was no way Angel would forgive her and Asjiah was the last person she could count on as a friend. She knew she wouldn't go against her brother. The bond the two of them shared was unbreakable, they were like some monstrous pair of pit bulls; bred to fight and protect their owners, which in their case meant each other.

The shrill sound of her phone ringing almost made her scream. Her hand shook as she flipped open the receiver and waited for the caller to speak.

"Hello?"

"*You have a collect call from:* Angel Cappelli."

Fear gripped her heart as she listened to him say his name.

"Press five to accept, or simply hang up to deny the call."

What was she supposed to do? Did he know? What if he didn't? If she hung up she would be admitting her guilt.

The automated voice repeated the greeting again, pausing momentarily while Stacey made her decision.

She quickly shut the phone and tossed it back on the bed as if it was covered in some foreign contaminant. She wanted to accept the call and take a chance that he might be willing to hear her confession but something inside of her said there wasn't enough Hail Mary's in the world that could save her.

The queen size bed cradled his six foot frame as he rolled over on his right side cursing the mattress for not being more comfortable. Unable to fall back asleep he clicked on the TV flicking through the channels until he found Sports Center. His dreams of playing basketball had fallen by the wayside and he wondered if he would ever make it to college.

STRIPPING ASJIAH

He could still apply, he had decent grades upon graduating high school so he was sure he could get in but he wasn't ready to leave. He had unfinished business to attend to, loose ends to tie up before he could begin to make plans for their future.

"Fuck."

He ran his hand over his chiseled abs, closed his eyes, and tried to will her out of his mind. But he couldn't. She was everywhere he turned; everywhere he looked, in his dreams, his subconscious, in his heart. He needed to move on, to forget about her.

Instead he remembered the last time he saw her, the last time he touched her, smelled her, and heard her laugh. He remembered their first kiss, how her lips felt against his, how she looked at him, and the sound of her voice.

Wasn't she the one who left him; without as much as a goodbye, farewell, a cheesy Hallmark card, or a voicemail? There was that one time that she did call but he ignored it out of fear that he wouldn't know what to say. His dismissal allowed her to believe he didn't want to talk to her and because of that, she hadn't called back.

So what was keeping him from calling her?

"This is stupid." Snatching his cell phone off the nightstand he started to dial her number at the same time his caller ID displayed a private call.

"Who is this?" Agitation seeped through the phone as he waited for the caller to identify themselves.

"You have a prepaid call, you will not be charged for this call. This call is from: Gabriel Torez."

"Gabe?"

"Press five to accept the call, or, simply hang up to deny the call."

BY SA'RESE

He pressed the corresponding key and waited for the call to be connected.

"My nigga," Dragging the first part of his greeting Gabe smiled as he thought of the expression the boy must've had on his face.

"What's up?"

"Plans changed. It's time for you to pay us a visit."

Bear was barking ferociously as he ran into my room. He sniffed around the couch in my sitting area, near the attic door, and inside my closet where he lingered for a minute.

The top drawer to my dresser, where I kept all my panties and bras was open.

Someone had been in here.

Very meticulous about how I fold my clothes it didn't take long to see that someone had rambled through my things.

I could feel my palms begin to sweat as I held up a pair of thongs which felt slightly damp. Tossing them onto the floor, I looked around my closet to see if anything else had been touched but nothing else seemed out of place.

From inside my bedroom, Bear began to bark again causing me to jump.

"What the fuck?"

A chill went down my spine as I looked at my bed. My black sheets were wrinkled and spattered with semen. I felt the lump begin to grow as I fought hard against the bile that was rising in my throat.

It couldn't be.

It wasn't possible.

He was here.

STRIPPING ASJIAH

Bear was on his hind legs, growling viciously at the window which was wide open.

I didn't have time to panic. I ran into the other room, grabbed every suitcase and overnight bag I owned and began packing.

I opened the She-Ra Cloud Castle that was in the very back of my closet and stuffed the rolls of money I had stashed inside of it into my book bag.

After making several trips to the car I went back upstairs to make sure I had gotten everything. There were still toys that I managed to salvage from California but I didn't have any room, I would have to come back and get those things later.

There was no way I would spend another night in this house. I had been a fool to think that I could come back here; careless to believe that I could let my guard down and that I would be safe here.

Descending the stairs three at a time I grabbed my purse off the kitchen table and ran out the side door with Bear following me. After he jumped in, I strapped the seatbelt around the Rottweiler and rushed over to the driver side.

Putting the Civic in reverse, I hoisted myself up with my left foot, placed my hand over the passenger side headrest, and backed out the driveway.

Bear barked again as he panted anxiously in the passenger seat.

"It's okay, boy. We're gonna go somewhere safe."

Had I taken a moment to look back at the house I would've seen what he was barking at.

Cash was on the roof, watching my every move.

BY SA'RESE

Chapter Seventeen

She couldn't breathe. Her efforts to free herself had failed and she was running out of time. It seemed the harder she fought, the tighter his grip became. Her lungs were on fire and pretty soon the oxygen that flowed to her heart would be cut off and she'd die.

She begged, pleaded for him to stop, to let her go but her cries fell on deaf ears.

He had no regard for human life. His eyes were filled with pure malice as he looked down at her. The vodka bottle that he shoved up her ass had caused her to bleed and that only angered him further. He punched her repeatedly, shouted curses, only stopping to change the position he had her in so that he could think of some other sick way to rape her.

What was taking so long? Why wouldn't she die? The mixture of blood and alcohol along with the bacterial infection she already had was causing the burning inside of her vagina to intensify.

She screamed but he thought it was out of pleasure so he didn't stop. He assumed the wetness he felt was from her arousal so he plunged his fist inside of her desperate to make her think it was his penis although his erection had failed him hours ago.

Her vision became blurry, the room seemed to shift, her eyes closed and she blacked out.

Finally, it was over.

"Hey." Danielle smiled and brushed Keyshia's hair out of her face.

"You're awake."

"You…"

"She's been here everyday with you since you were admitted."

Ashley walked over to the bed, pressed a button on the remote, and adjusted the pillow so she could sit up.

"You were there, in the bathroom…"

"Yes, I called the ambulance. My name's Danielle but everyone calls me Danny."

Keyshia looked at the girl who had saved her life and began to cry.

"Aww, don't do that. It's okay, you're all better now." Danielle took one of the tissues and affectionately wiped her face.

"I'm sorry, it's just that…well I…I thought…"

"You don't have to apologize; you have every right to be emotional."

"Thank you."

"Did you buy me all this?" Keyshia looked around the room motioning at the stuffed animals and balloons.

"No, it's from Asjiah."

"Asjiah?"

"Yeah, you had her listed as your sister in your phone so I called her. She came up here a few minutes later and then got into it with your mom."

"My mother was here?"

"Yep and things got pretty heated between them."

"I bet."

"She has quite the temper on her; I thought your mom was going to hit her."

"Damn, it was like that? She could only imagine what her mother must've thought let alone the things that probably ran through Asjiah's mind when they saw her.

"Yeah, but she didn't back down. She holds her own to be so small."

Keyshia rolled her eyes at the way she was glorifying Asjiah.

"She's all bark and no bite, don't let her scare you."

Danielle folded the blanket that had kept her warm through the night and continued to ramble.

"She's very pretty."

"Who?"

"Asjiah," Danielle thought back to their first encounter two weeks ago. She looked mixed. With what she wasn't sure but she was beautiful. Thick black curls cascaded down her back and her buttermilk complexion was kissed with freckles that seemed to be placed perfectly on her face and those eyes; such pretty blue eyes.

The clicking sound of Keyshia sucking her tongue in annoyance snapped her out of her daydream.

"She's aiight."

"She was worried about you. She comes up here just about every night and brings you something from the gift shop."

"She can't be too worried if you're here and she isn't."

"I don't know what's going on between the two of you but you should talk to her, and work things out."

"You sure have a lot of opinions given the fact you don't know me, Asjiah, or the situation." Keyshia winced as she leaned on her elbow.

"What did you say your name was again?"

"Danielle."

"What school did you go to? Where did you grow up?"

STRIPPING ASJIAH

"Warrensville and I grew up off Northfield, lived in Granada Apartments, anything else?"

First she was questioned by Asjiah now this. Why were they so unappreciative? If it weren't for her, she would've died in that room, alone and by herself.

"So Danielle from Warrensville, do you always poke your nose into other people's affairs?" Keyshia grimaced once more as she reached for the cup of water next to her bed.

"My nose saved your life. If it weren't for me you'd be laying on a slab somewhere being filled with embalming fluid."

The tension was thick. For a minute the girls eyes were locked in an intense stare, both challenging each other silently, neither looking away until one of them spoke.

"You know I saw him." Danielle got up from Keyshia's bed and sat in the chair crossing her arms as if to say 'now what'.

"Saw who?"

She felt paralyzed; fear was causing her to reminisce of the time she spent locked up in that room. Vivid pictures of blood, her blood, the shrill sound of screams, and his animal like grunting.

Bringing her out of her thoughts, Danielle continued to talk, "The man who was in the room with you, the person who I assume, did this to you."

"I don't know what you're talking about."

"Big black guy, bald head, about six feet or taller,"

Keyshia couldn't recall what he looked like, he had to have been attractive enough for her to agree to go to a hotel with him but her memory was hazy, his description was fragmented pieces in her subconscious, everything except...

"And he had this scar on his neck."

That.

BY SA'RESE

The machine to the left of the bed began to beep rapidly signaling a spike in her heart rate. Keyshia clutched her gown, gasping for breath.

"Nurse!"

Climbing back into the house, Cash closed the window behind him and sat down on the bed. Running his hands over his bald head he tried to hold on to her image as long as he could. It was hard for him to contain himself as he watched her rush through her room terrified that her worst fear was materializing.

She had noticed her clothes had been tampered with, she had seen the sheets; she knew it was him. He didn't mean to alarm her; he only wanted her to become aware of his presence to let her know that her act of vengeance wouldn't go unpunished. But she ran. Where he was uncertain but he was sure in due time he would find her and fate would bring them back together again. Until then he waited.

STRIPPING ASJIAH

Chapter Eighteen

"Pooh Bear!"

I heard her voice before her small, petite figure appeared in the doorway. She had affectionately nick named me Pooh when I was born because she said I looked like the Disney character as a baby; fat, soft and cuddly.

Her vanilla colored skin was smooth and radiant and a head full of curly gray hair was all over her head. Behind reading glasses, one blue and one gray eye beamed back at me with excitement. Time hadn't aged her at all; she still looked the same from when I was a little girl. She was by far the cutest little lady I knew.

"Hi Grandma-me," She smelled like baby powder as I hugged her I immediately began to feel better.

Bear stood beside me patiently waiting for her to acknowledge him as well. A gentle rub behind the ears was enough to satisfy him as he trotted by us into the house.

In between the times that my father waited to be stationed somewhere else with the Army, we would always come back here and stay with her until we got housing. Given that this was his side of the family and where I spent the better years of my childhood, I felt more comfortable around her. That and the fact I looked more like my father's family. I didn't have to worry about people playing the "name that child" game when someone came to visit.

Unfortunately things were the opposite for Angel and since everyone on this side was damn near white, he would stick out like a sore thumb. The difference is no one ever treated him like

BY SA'RESE

he didn't belong. Unlike Marie, they didn't see color. They loved us because we were my parent's children and most of all because we were family.

If I would've had things my way I would've preferred for Grandma-me to be my guardian. I'm sure shit would've been a lot different.

"My little Pooh, what are you doing here? It's not the weekend yet is it?"

I sat my things near the stairs then joined her in the living room.

"No, it's not the weekend yet. I missed you and I wanted to come and stay with you for a while."

She pushed her glasses up on her nose, "You know you can stay here as long as you like."

Trying not to appear shaken I grabbed her hand and held it against my cheek before kissing it. "I know."

"So what shall we do first?"

I pretended to think of an activity for us although I already knew what I wanted.

"Can we make cookies?"

Baking was something that she had been doing with me since I was a toddler. We would be up to our elbows in chocolate chips and cookie dough and afterwards, she would always let me lick the bowl.

While the cookies were in the oven, we would have tea and sit and talk about anything my little heart desired. Of course my conversation skills had improved since I was three but our tradition hadn't changed.

Scratching Bears ears she talked to him as he stared back at her attentively. "Pooh said she wants cookies, so let's go make cookies."

STRIPPING ASJIAH

I got up and followed them into the kitchen and it wasn't long before I allowed the aroma of melting chocolate to invade my senses and erase my thoughts of Cash.

"The nurse said you had a panic attack."

Keyshia was hoping it was all a bad dream but when she opened her eyes, the little Latina girl was still sitting in the chair and she was still in the hospital.

Danielle's admission had sent her into a state of anxiety, of dread, vertigo, in which it became difficult for her to breathe thus causing her little episode.

She didn't want to believe there was any truth to her statement but after she described his scar, the scar she seen over and over in her dreams, she knew she wasn't lying.

Danielle refilled Keyshia's glass of water then sat down on the edge of the bed.

"Look, I don't know what your situation is but I've been here with you, everyday for two weeks now and from the looks of things your mother isn't coming back so aside from Asjiah, you don't have anyone else. So why don't we start over. You tell me a little about yourself, I'll tell you a little about me and maybe when you feel comfortable, you can tell me what happened to you."

She wanted to be mad at somebody, blame anybody for what had happened but all fingers pointed back at her. Danielle was right; she didn't have anyone to turn to. She hadn't spoken to Asjiah since their last talk in the library; she definitely couldn't face her now, what would she think of her? What would she say? Looking back, Asjiah had tried to warn her, but she mistook her words of caution as jealousy.

BY SA'RESE

Keyshia blinked several times attempting to keep the tears from falling.

"I guess I should start from the beginning."

"How far along are you?"

Coughing, I tried not to spill cranberry-apple tea all over myself. Her question caught me off guard and I had to pat myself on the chest to keep from choking.

"How did you know?" I rubbed my eyes which had begun to water as a result of my coughing.

Grandma-me giggled as she got up from the chair and patted my swollen abdomen. "Little Pooh kicked me when I hugged you earlier."

I placed my hand over hers and leaned my head against her chest. "I'm scared."

"Now, now; you're a strong girl Asjiah. A lot stronger than you give yourself credit for. You've been through worse things before and this baby is a blessing. You may not understand it now, but this child may be exactly what you need to help you heal."

"I almost had an abortion; I don't deserve to be a mother."

This time my eyes were filled with real tears as I thought back to my experience at the clinic.

"I was going to kill it. I was going to murder my baby."

"Hush now." Wrapping her arms around me she kissed me on the forehead. "You were just scared that's all. Everything's going to be okay. I'll help you as best I can."

I would've never gotten this reaction out of Marie. She was still unaware of my pregnancy and I'm sure the minute I told her she would call me all kinds of dumb bitches, sluts, and whatever else she could think of. Grandma-me, on the other hand, consoled me, spoke to me in a soothing tone and reassured me that everything would be fine. She trusted me to make the right decisions and if I did make a mistake, we talked about it and she allowed me room to learn from it, and see, the error in my ways.

Bear began to snore prompting laughter from both of us as we looked down at his gigantic body sprawled out on the floor. I could tell he felt more comfortable here as well.

"So do you have names picked out?"

"No. Not yet. I don't know what I'm having so I've just been calling it baby Jai."

"She would like that."

We shared a brief moment of silence for my mother until the familiar dinging noise of the timer sounded letting us know that the cookies were done. I retrieved two small saucers from the cabinet as she got the baking sheet out of the oven. I placed one cookie on each plate and handed them to her while I carried our tea cups back into the living room.

As I took my place across from her I looked out the window and watched as the sun faded behind the trees. I was only fifteen minutes away from Marie's house but when I was here, it felt like we were worlds apart.

I awoke the next morning curled up in the chair covered in one of her hand knitted quilts. I don't remember falling asleep or at what time I dozed off, but being pregnant had finally caught up to me and my body shut down.

My mind was usually overflowing with all kinds of miscellaneous thoughts but last night I didn't dream at all. Instead I allowed the constant beat of a tiny little heart to play a lullaby in my ears that eventually sung me to sleep.

BY SA'RESE

In the kitchen I could hear the clanging of pots and pans, mixed in with the sizzling of bacon, and Grandma-me humming. The scent of oatmeal sent a wave of nausea through my body and within seconds I was on my knees hugging the toilet.

I didn't have an extreme case of morning sickness like most girls but of course there were certain things I couldn't eat or tolerate the smell of.

After spitting up parts of the cookies I ate last night, I brushed my teeth, coiled my hair into a bun, and went into the kitchen where a cup of tea was waiting for me.

"This should make you feel better."

She handed me a plate with bacon, scrambled cheese eggs, and a cranberry muffin. Grandma-me took a seat across from me and stirred the bowl of oats that had caused me to vomit moments before. I covered my mouth as the familiar queasy feeling began to fester in my stomach.

"Oh Pooh Bear, I'm sorry." She got up and dumped the oatmeal back into the pot trading it for the same thing she had just fixed for me.

Laughing I rubbed my stomach as the baby began to calm down. "I guess I should've told you all the things little pooh doesn't like."

"It's okay, I can eat that later. How did you sleep?"

"Pretty good actually, I was really tired."

"I could tell. I started to wake you so you could go upstairs to your room but you looked so peaceful."

She stirred her tea in silence then cleared her throat.

"Are you okay Asjiah?

It was almost as if someone had pulled a light switch inside of my head and the dark room where I stored the things I tried to forget suddenly became illuminated for everyone to see.

STRIPPING ASJIAH

"I can't go back there."

"Go back where sweetie?"

"To Marie's house," I knew if I looked in her eyes long enough I would begin to cry so I picked up our dishes and carried them over to the sink.

"She doesn't want me there anyway, so why should I stay somewhere that I'm not wanted?"

"If someone has hurt you Asjiah, I need to know."

Flashbacks of my rape began to replay in my mind and I wanted to tell her what happened. I wanted her to have some special wand that would make everything okay but I knew she didn't. I walked over to her, kissed her on the cheek, and lied.

"I'm okay; I would just rather be here with you."

If I told her the truth I knew she would call the police. I also knew they wouldn't catch him. Even if they did, jail wasn't enough to appease the pain he had caused me. I harbored so much hate towards him, so many ill feelings.

I wanted a more severe punishment than any jury could ever grant him, I wanted him to experience something far worse than what might happen to him in prison. I wanted his life. And now that I knew he was alive, if given a second chance, I was going to take it.

After breakfast I got dressed and began my hour long journey to Mansfield to see Angel. As I drove, the sun seemed to race above me behind trees that had begun to shed their leaves a sign of winter's approach.

Three bathroom breaks later, I pulled into the parking lot.

I noticed the warm rays that had danced throughout the sky just moments ago, now gave way to dismal clouds that loomed over the prison.

BY SA'RESE

I was glad to see that the tacky guard, who was there the first time I visited, wasn't in attendance. I didn't have the energy to put up with his weak ass pick up lines and I was sure if I smelled his breath, I would throw up in his face.

I went through all the formalities and soon found myself waiting to be buzzed in through the huge metal door that would then lead me across a small courtyard and into the visiting room.

The C.O. that questioned my relationship to Angel kept his eyes glued to the newspaper he was reading as I approached the sign in desk. I was certain Angel had exchanged words with him, now he was afraid to talk to me. It was crazy that although he was the one being detained, he still put fear into people's hearts.

I followed the same routine as before and after getting snacks out of the vending machine I found a place in the corner for us to sit.

"Little baby,"

I was afraid that baby Jai would move as Angel hugged me tightly. I wasn't ready to tell him I was pregnant yet.

"How are you?" He looked just as neat and well kept as the last time I saw him.

"I'm straight, what's up with you?"

"Actually I need to tell you something."

The entire drive up here I was debating on whether or not I should tell Angel about Cash. I didn't want to upset him or cause him to worry but then again, he had the right to know that this fucking creep wasn't dead.

"Cash is alive."

I could tell he was grinding his teeth by the way his jaw moved, the wrinkles in his forehead let me know that he wasn't too pleased with the news.

"What?"

STRIPPING ASJIAH

"He was in my room."

Angel ran his hands across his face and sat back in his chair. "You saw him?"

"No. When I got home after coming to see you last time, I heard someone walking around upstairs but by the time I got up the courage to go up there, whoever it was, was gone."

Angel put his head down and closed his eyes for a second before looking back up at me.

"Then how do you know it was him?"

"Seriously, who else could it had been Angel? That nasty son-of-a-bitch was in my closet doing who knows what to my clothes, and he nutted in my bed." I shivered slightly at the thought of his semen splattered all over my sheets.

"So where did he go?"

"I don't know. One of my windows was open but I wasn't about to stick around and try to look for him so I packed all my shit up, took Bear, and went over Grandma-me's house."

I looked over at my brother and I knew he was thinking the same thing that had ran through my mind. How the hell could he be alive?

"I'm gonna call Caleb and let him know where you're staying."

"C'mon Angel, I don't need a babysitter."

"Look, as long as that nigga is somewhere out in the streets, I'm not gonna be satisfied unless I have people that I can trust watching out for you."

"People?"

Angel waved his hand and dismissed my comment. "Just do what I say A'!" Heads turned our way as his voice rose.

"I can't let anything happen to you."

I discreetly ran my hand across my stomach as the baby shifted. I had more to think about than just myself now.

"Fine,"

Angel's eyes went cold as he looked at me. "As much as I would love to handle that bitch myself, I can't touch him from in here. Just know that Caleb will have the go ahead to murk that nigga on sight if he has to."

"Okay."

He slouched slightly in his chair and I could tell from his body language that his attitude was back to normal.

"Now listen up because I gotta lot of shit to tell you in a small amount of time so pay attention."

I felt like I should've brought a notebook and a pen to take notes but I didn't want him to think I was incapable of handling the responsibility he was giving me so I cleared my thoughts and relied on my memory to file away everything he was getting ready to say.

"Pretty much the shit is just basic math. A bird is no less than 1,008 grams but the one's I get are 1,022. They usually go for anything from $16-24,000 a key but this part isn't really that important because you'll always pay seventeen flat. Ounces are $800, half is $400, a quarter is $200 and a ball is $100."

Angel took a sip from his juice then looked at me to make sure I was still with him.

"Make sense so far?"

"Yeah, it makes sense."

"Shit isn't hard to run; you just have to have your mind and your people right. In your case, the pieces have already been placed on the board; you just have to make the right moves."

"Like chess?"

"Exactly,"

STRIPPING ASJIAH

Normally Angel's analogies or metaphors sounded like broken Dr. Seuss poems but when he talked about drugs, you would think he had written a manual.

I waited patiently as he took a bite out of the turkey sandwich, wiped his mouth, and then continued.

"Don't worry about shit on the streets, Caleb will help you out on that end and pretty soon someone else will come into the picture to smooth things out."

I wanted to interject and ask him who this "someone else" was but I knew he would just keep talking in riddles and not give me a straight answer.

"Seriously A', if you don't get it, or you have a question, just ask me."

I stuffed some chips in my mouth and waved my hand for him to continue. "I'm good."

"If you need to, find a couple of gullible ass dudes and use them to be your holders and movers. Buy a couple of book bags, and when you're about to make a move; small or big, use them as pawns. Your holders should be the ones touching the dope, not you. Not unless you have to re-up. That should be the only major time you're involved."

"Am I gonna have to cut it?"

"Good question little baby." Angel smiled as if he was a teacher and I was his star pupil. "You're gonna give it to them soft. By the time it gets up our way, it's already been stepped on."

"Oh, ok."

"So to me, a smart muthafucka would just bust it down and sell it. Let the buyers fuck it up at their own risk. One thing they will know is that they screwed it up and not you." Angel put his hand together so they were touching at the fingertips. He looked me dead in my eyes and the tone in his voice got more serious.

"This shit's a business A', I'm not on no fuck shit when I say this but don't get caught up with these lame ass niggas and don't put them on to shit."

I broke the seal on my bottle of water and drank some before addressing him.

"I'm not on these cornball ass little boys so you don't have to worry about that. Besides, half of them are scared to talk to me because they know I'm your sister."

"Good. Let them know that I'll beat the fucking brakes off they ass if they try some shit." His eyebrows wrinkled up as they always did when he got angry.

"Now like I was saying, the reason why a lot of people don't make it in the game is because they live out of their means. Just because you're making money don't mean you have to be flashy."

I laughed as I remembered one of my favorite movies. "That's why ol' boy and his wife got popped in Goodfellas; buying new cars, fur coats and shit."

Angel's mood lightened up for a second as he smiled at me and laughed.

"Right, I could've been out there pushing Benz's n' shit but things like that bring unwanted attention. All the more reason I bought you something simple like a Civic. It's a cute little girlie car, nothing that you wouldn't have bought or couldn't have been given to you as a gift, feel me?"

"Yeah,"

"If you do choose to kick it or go out, do it somewhere else. Go to Columbus, down to Cincinnati, or someplace like that. Don't try to be Ms. Party all the time either. You're only doing this so you won't have to depend on anyone for shit. I'm not always going to be there so I need to know that you're able to take care of yourself. All those runs I used to let you go on, all the times I used to let you watch me bag shit up, it was all for this moment. Use this as a stepping stone to start a business or something. Or use it to pay your way through college. Be smart about it so eventually you won't have to do what you're doing to get money."

His eyes softened as he brushed my hair behind my ear. He looked as if he wanted to say something else; to tell me he was sorry that we were in this situation but now wasn't the time for emotions or weakness.

"I know I don't have to tell you this but if you get caught, don't say shit. No matter what kind of time they're trying to throw at you, no matter what kind of deal they're trying to offer you, don't talk. Loose lips sink ships, remember that."

I grabbed his hand before he moved it away from my face and held it. "I'll be fine."

"Alright, time's up!"

The correctional officers began to circulate through the room in an effort to wrap up everyone's visits and get the inmates back to their cells.

"And just like that it's over huh?" I brushed off my jeans and stood up.

"I guess so. Don't worry; I'll be home soon enough."

"I miss you Angel." My hormones were all over the place and I silently cursed myself as I hugged him and my eyes began to tear up.

"Don't go crying on me little baby. You're my sister so I know you'll be okay. And don't let that nigga Cash throw you off your shit. You're a Cappelli, we run from no man."

Angel kissed my cheek and as I watched him walk away, I had a new found respect for my brother. Sure he had dropped out of high school but he had a certain kind of intelligence that you couldn't teach in a classroom or find in a book. He was a business man in every since of the word and I was his apprentice.

Chapter Nineteen

"Wow."

Danielle wiped her face trying to rid herself of the horrifying picture that Keyshia had just painted for her. She had told her everything starting with Vale and how she got turned onto threesomes and coke by him and his boy, the talk she had with Asjiah in the library, her sex tape and all the events in between that ultimately led up to her being in the hospital.

"I'm so sorry."

"Don't be. It was the life I chose, and the decisions I made that started all of this. I have no one to blame but myself."

"So you have no idea who the guy was that attacked you?" Keyshia was silent for a minute before continuing. "No. I had never seen him before that day. I just hate to think that he's still out there. What if he knows I'm alive? What if he knows that I'm in here?"

"Do you have anywhere to stay? Are you planning on going home once you're released from here?"

She chuckled and looked at her new friend, "You met my mother, would you go home to someone like that?"

Danielle laughed, "Nah, I guess I wouldn't." She took a minute to think about her offer before she put it on the table. Over the past few hours a bond had been formed between them and in a sense she felt responsible for her. God had placed her in her life for a reason and perhaps that reason was to look after her.

"You can stay with me if you want."

BY SA'RESE

Keyshia was shocked and confused all at the same time. What had she done to deserve such kindness? This girl had been by her bedside from the moment she found her and now she was offering her someplace to live? Her eyes watered with tears of joy as she began to cry.

"Come on, don't do that. You're gonna make me think that you're the one that's all bark and no bite and not Asjiah."

Both girls laughed as Keyshia cleaned her face up.

"Seriously, my boyfriend is always in and out of town so you don't have to worry about him, it would be nice having someone around, besides we have an extra room anyway so you're more than welcome. You'd also have your own bathroom so you don't have to worry about that either."

"I mean, as long as you're cool with it, I don't want to crowd your space."

"Girl please; no worries. It'll be fun."

"What'll be fun?" Walking into the room I casually sat down in the chair and looked at them; taken aback by how close they seemed to be.

"I see you're still here." I half heartedly waved at Danielle then turned my attention to Keyshia. "Well hello Sleeping Beauty."

"A', I...I,"

"You what, didn't expect me to be here? I was here almost every day when you were first admitted or didn't our little friend tell you that?"

Before she could respond I got up and walked over to her so I could get a better look at her face.

"The surgeons did a really good job, minimal scarring, you're healing up really well. I'm glad you're doing better."

STRIPPING ASJIAH

Keyshia looked up at me with glazed eyes, "I thought you hated me, I thought you were coming here to gloat and give me a bunch of I told you so's."

I was really beginning to despise my hormones and how baby Jai was making me super sensitive, I soon found myself fighting back tears.

"Who told you that? Keesh the last time we spoke we argued, we had opposing views, and you wanted to do something that I didn't want to be a part of. We both have really strong personalities so I didn't bother arguing with you. When I saw that tape I just felt like it was nothing I could do for you at that point. You were too far beyond my reach. I'm sorry things turned out the way that they did but I love you. No matter what happens, nothing will ever change that."

Keyshia extended her arms to hug me and I returned her embrace. For a moment we forgot Danielle was in the room until we heard her sniffling. We both looked at her and burst out laughing.

"Now what were you two talking about before I got here?"

"Danielle told me that I can stay with her until I get back on my feet."

Still unsure of what role she played in all of this I turned to her eyebrow raised. "Oh did you? That's very nice."

Sensing where I was going with this Keyshia cut me off.

"She's cool A'. We talked and I told her everything."

"She told me about her attack and it seems like we saw the same person."

"What?" I was on the edge of my chair now. Danielle told me that she hadn't seen anyone when we were at the diner now all of a sudden she remembered who this nigga was?

"So you know him?" I looked from Keyshia back to Danielle waiting for them to shine some light on the situation.

"No, I don't remember his name but we both described the same person." Keyshia shuttered as she thought of her assailant.

"And?"

"He's a black guy, tall, dark skinned, bald head, and…"

I couldn't breathe. I felt like my heart stopped along with baby Jai's. This was impossible. My palms began to sweat and my leg started to shake. Before she could form another word I finished her sentence for her, "He has a scar across his neck."

Both girls looked at me petrified.

"How do you know him Asjiah?"

I joined them on the bed and tried to keep my composure, tears flooding my cheeks as all of the sordid details of my rape came back to the surface.

"Asjiah?"

"A' what's wrong?"

Danielle rubbed my back and Keyshia took my hand as they waited for me to say something. I looked from one girl to the other and allowed the cruel truth to spill out onto the sheets.

"He's my Uncle."

Chapter Twenty

If I could breathe my life into your lungs I would.

I'd leave this world and trade with you if that meant I could escape all the insanity around me. Selfless as it may seem I would be robbing you of your peace just so I could runaway and take refuge amongst the Angels.

I thought all the drama from last summer was over. I though that the only task before me was packing up my life and moving to Atlanta. I thought by now I would be miles and miles away from this shit. It seems like no matter how fast I run; my past is always right there with me waiting for me to get winded and stop so it could be the water that quenches my thirst. Regardless of how far I drive away, its there, taunting me in the rearview mirror reminding me that it's a lot closer than it appears.

If I had any doubts before, they were all put to rest after talking to Keyshia and Danielle.

I'm still trying to wrap my mind around the fact that Cash was responsible for her being in the hospital.

He almost killed her.

Was her mother right?

Was I to be held accountable for what happened?

No. I refused to allow myself to be burdened with that kind of guilt. I already carried around enough. I blamed myself for not being able to save you, for not being able to fight off Cash, for not protecting Angel all those nights he was beat. I couldn't add Keyshia to all of that. My shoulders weren't strong enough especially when so much was weighing me down already.

There was no way Cash knew Keyshia and I were acquainted; he never saw us together and she was never at Marie's house when he was. Their encounter had to be some kind of freakish coincidence.

I thought I would be afraid if and when I found out he was alive but I'm not. After seeing so much as a child, after being put through so many tribulations, complacency replaces what should be fear.

As sick as it may sound, I felt his presence. Some nights I would close my eyes and feel him breathing on me, the stench of Bacardi on his tongue as he licked my face.

What was he waiting for? Why didn't he stay in my room instead of running? What was he planning?

I couldn't let myself get thrown off or caught up in his thoughts. I didn't have time to entertain the "what if's" I refused to live constantly looking over my shoulders waiting for him to strike. If he wanted me, one way or another he would come get me.

Angel isn't around to protect me and I can't count on Caleb to come to my rescue when and if something does happen. Angel was all I had and now he's in prison for the next three years. The realization that all I have is me, well, that's kind of scary.

Last summer changed me. Granted my perception of life hasn't been the same since your absence but I feel like I have to fight so much harder now. I feel like I've been robbed of so *many things over the past ten years and I don't know what to do to get them back or if I can.*

My thoughts are different, the naiveté that comes with being a child, a teenager, all of that has escaped me. I feel like I'm growing up too fast. I wish these eighteen years would've been recorded; that I could rewind, and delete when necessary. I wouldn't have any use for the fast forward button, I don't want to see what lies ahead of me before it happens and I wouldn't voluntarily choose to live in the fast lane but unfortunately that's where I've ended up. A road filled with green lights, an occasional yield sign, and red lights scattered few and far between.

But I don't have time for weakness, no room for frailties, I have to be strong even in times when I don't want to and hope that the gluttons of the world don't eat me alive.

I told Keyshia and Danielle about Baby Jai. It was nice to get it out and actually be able to feel happy about my pregnancy verses arguing with CJ. Of course now they want to be all cutesy and throw me a baby shower. I wanted to tell them no but Keyshia needs a distraction so I gave them the go ahead to do whatever their little hearts desired.

All I want is to be with you. To go out shopping for baby stuff and ask you all my weird soon to be mommy questions. To look at you with complete admiration as I listen to you laugh while I complain about getting fat and all my weird cravings. But I can't.

Instead I smiled and appeared to be interested as they rambled excitedly about decorations, where we could have it, and who they would invite. I zoned out somewhere between toilet tissue and some other game involving the contents of our purse.

I was back in my bathroom at Grandma-me's house staring at my reflection, entranced by my eyes, his eyes. I find myself hypnotized by the darkness I saw looking back at me dancing wickedly in seas of blue. The coldness that chills my skin also warms my heart.

It's in that instant that I realize I'm happy Cash has resurrected, glad that he has decided to make his presence known, only so I can have the pleasure of killing him again.

I brushed the debris that had fallen from the tree off my jeans and did the same to my blanket before folding it. The Chrysanthemum's I had chosen blended perfectly with the colors of fall.

Tearing the entry out of my notebook, I rolled it up and placed it in the vase with the flowers. I knew that it would eventually blow away or disintegrate when it rained but I chose to believe that once I left God would grant her a brief amount of time to come down and retrieve it.

If I said that out loud to a shrink I would be committed for sure. It wasn't that I couldn't distinguish between what was real and what wasn't, in some cases I just chose not to.

STRIPPING ASJIAH

Chapter Twenty-One

Looking around the cafeteria sized visiting area; he quietly studied all the inmates. He watched as this country looking white boy kissed his girlfriend wondering what he had done to land him in prison. He looked like one of those wholesome farm kids that tended to the barn animals, went to church daily, and chewed straw while he helped his daddy throw hay onto the back of some old pick up truck.

He probably played high school sports, baseball most likely; and was guaranteed a full ride to some Ivy League school until he fucked it up. His guess was that during training camp, all the jocks threw a little party and some chic decided at the last minute that letting the entire team hit home runs wasn't such a good idea. The situation turned ugly, she got raped, and now he was in jail. What he really wanted to know was if his girl knew that her boyfriend was now his cellmates bat boy.

Money's eyes wandered to another couple; this time an elderly white male in his mid forties who was sitting across from some woman he presumed to be his wife. This one was easy. Clean shaven, blue collar, upper class white man; he had embezzlement or money laundering written all over him. He looked like he could've been a lawyer, the sleazy type, like that grease ball off of Carlito's Way.

He most likely washed money and created off shore accounts for his big name clientele but somewhere along the way, he probably got greedy, started getting sloppy and forgot to cover his tracks.

He began to analyze the bi-racial boy to his far right when someone interrupted his thoughts.

BY SA'RESE

"I'm thinking he used to be that nigga on the outside, dope boy of course, probably had all the girls on him since he got that pretty boy thing going on. My guess is murder."

"Okay, okay, I can see that" Money took a second to give the boy a once over then gave his opinion.

"I'm thinking he gets locked up, decides to bring out his sweet side, but everybody in here is too scared to say shit about it because of his reputation on the streets."

Caleb began to laugh as he shook Money's hand and pulled up a chair.

"What's been up with you?"

"Shit, the usual. Trying to figure out what's going on here." Money brushed off his Evisu jeans and continued to survey his surroundings.

"How long you been back?"

"A couple days,"

Caleb used the corner of his t-shirt to wipe off the pop can before opening it, "You see yo' girl yet?"

Money knew who he was referring to but he didn't feel like talking about her.

"And who is that?"

"Oh you fronting now?" Caleb smirked as he took a sip of his soda. "You know who I'm talking bout dude; Asjiah."

The sound of her name made his heart flutter. She had been all he thought about on his drive back into Cleveland. He wanted to call her but he didn't. He was going to stop by her people's house and see her but he was sure she was in Atlanta by now.

"Nah, I haven't seen her."

Caleb was hoping he would say that so he could antagonize him.

"Well I have. And shit…"

STRIPPING ASJIAH

"You've seen her?"

"Yeah she didn't go to ATL she's…"

"…Staying off of Lee Road on Clearview,"

Money and Caleb turned towards the voice then immediately got up to greet their friends. Money hadn't seen Angel or Gabriel since last summer and it didn't look like prison had changed them at all. Gabe's hair had grown into this wild, unruly afro and they both looked like they had been hitting the yard.

He wasn't sure if he should be mad at Angel for the gamble he had taken with his life or if he should just chalk it up as it being part of the game. That day could've turned out a lot differently than Angel had anticipated and it could've easily been him and Caleb behind bars. He wasn't afraid of being in jail but he would've rather been aware of the odds before he decided to take that trip.

"I guess you're wondering why you're here." Angel unwrapped the turkey sandwich and began to dress it with the condiments he had asked for.

"Asjiah has been given the reigns of my operation. As I suspected, she's taken the knowledge I dropped on her and flipped it in her own little way. Caleb confirmed my suspicions and from what he's told me, she's found a way to make twice as much as I was making when I was on the streets." Angel wiped the corners of his mouth and smiled like a proud father.

"Caleb has been managing things around the way and although he's been holding shit down, he has also been asked to keep an eye on my sister. I can't expect him to do everything by himself so that's where you come in."

Money kept his eyes focused on Angel and his breathing even. He wasn't sure what was going to be asked of him, but he was ready for anything.

BY SA'RESE

"You still got what I gave you right?"

"Yeah,"

"Hold on to it. Asjiah's gonna need to re-up eventually and you already have it so that prevents her from having to really put her hands on anything. I also want you to watch her."

Angel paused for a second so he could read Money's body language and facial expression. He was impressed to see that he didn't waiver under pressure.

"I know you got feelings for my sister and what not, so now I'm entrusting you with her life. If anything happens to her, I swear to God, I will kill you."

Money didn't flinch or blink an eye. He knew how much Asjiah meant to him just as well as he knew his threat wasn't a threat at all but a promise.

"There's something else too." Angel didn't want to burden them with any more bad news but they needed to know about Cash in case they ran into him.

"Cash is alive."

This was the first time Gabe had heard Angel talk about his uncle. He thought they had taken care of everything. He witnessed what had gone down first hand so how was this dude still living? Out of the corner of his eye he could see that Caleb had the same look of bewilderment on his face.

"Who is Cash?" Money looked around the circle curious about who this person was and why everyone suddenly seemed so shook.

"My uncle," Angel ran his hands across his face and put his head down.

Sensing his frustration, Gabe stepped in before Angel got too upset.

"He raped Asjiah last summer."

STRIPPING ASJIAH

As soon as the words left Gabe's lips Money wished he could've taken his question back. Asjiah had been raped? Why didn't he know about this? His emotions began to get the best of him and before he could get a grip on his thoughts, he spoke.

"Why the fuck is this nigga still alive? You let this muthafucka rape yo' sister and you sitting here telling me this dude is still breathing? What kind of sick shit are you on?"

Caleb grabbed Money by the arm and urged him to calm down. "Chill out."

"Chill out; man, get yo' fucking hands off me!"

"Caleb's right Money, calm down." Gabe was in as much shock to hear this news as everyone else was but he wasn't expecting Money to react this way.

"Why are we sitting here talking about this shit instead of trying to find him?"

"Because he's going to come to us," Angel lifted his head and to everyone's surprise, appeared calm.

"When I found out what he had done to A' I handled it, or at least I thought I did. But when Asjiah came to visit a couple of weeks ago, she told me that he had paid her a visit."

Money interrupted again, this time targeting Caleb. "Where the fuck were you? Aren't you supposed to be watching her?"

Angel held his hand up silencing Money. "She didn't see him, but he had been in her room. From what she told me, our dog was with her, so had Cash actually tried to confront her, Bear would've eaten him alive."

Some of the tension seemed to disappear off of Money's face now that he knew Asjiah had gotten away unscathed.

"I don't know how the fuck he survived, but if either of you run into this nigga, kill him." Angel's eyes bore an expression of pure malevolence as he gave his boys permission to murder his mother's brother.

"He's about 6'1" maybe taller, dark-skinned, bald head, and he should have a scar across his neck where A' cut him."

"What did you mean when you said he should come to us?" Caleb could only imagine how pissed Cash had to be given what they had done to him.

"He's a dope head; I used to sell to him, so when he finds out my product is still on the streets, I'm sure he will find you."

Gabe hated that he couldn't be on the other side of these walls in the middle of the action and from the way Angel was seething he could tell he felt the same way.

It seemed like hours passed by as the group of friends remained prisoners of their own thoughts.

"Next time y'all lil nigga's come up in here, bring a bitch with you. I'm tired of looking at this nigga all day."

Caleb almost choked on his pop from Gabe's sudden outburst.

"Dude be in here all oiled up n'shit posing for prison flicks to send these mail order hoes he be writing." Gabe flexed his arms and imitated Angel causing the group to burst into more hysterics.

"You just hating cause the ladies love me." Angel touched his goatee and rubbed his hair as if he was admiring himself in the mirror.

"I'm not hating I'm just saying; I'd prefer to look at some chic with a fat ass rather than my homeboy doing pushups."

Although they had managed to lighten the mood, laughter wouldn't allow Money to ignore the one thing that lays dormant in his mind; Asjiah.

STRIPPING ASJIAH

Chapter Twenty-Two

I was never feeling the whole Cleveland State thing Angel was trying to sell me, I only sat there and listened to him yack about it because I knew that's what he wanted me to do. Nothing was wrong with CSU but I had no interest in going there, it was never one of my choices, had it been then I would've applied.

Besides, there was no way I would be able to stay focused in class, while pregnant, and do what he was asking at the same time. I didn't want my first year of college to reflect a poor G.P.A and screw up my transcripts so I had to come up with a different plan.

I wanted to go to Clark and come hell or high water that's where I was going to go. So in the meantime, I would sit out and find a way to do what Angel asked of me. I just needed to think outside the box.

Next Urban Gear; a clothing store in Randall Park Mall, turned out to be the perfect cover up and it wasn't long before I had the place clicking. At three months I still wasn't showing and even if I was, when I applied, the manager spent more time looking at my breasts than at my work experience so I doubt if it would've mattered.

The majority of the employees were girls so I already knew what kind of operation he was running. I was supposed to be 'store candy' so to speak, to bring in business and flirt with the customers to get them to buy the merchandise; little did he know I would be selling more than clothes.

At first I bumped into a few dudes that I went to high school with and after picking out a couple of outfits for them, they would ask about my brother. Most of them had already given up on asking me out so they got straight to the point; they wanted me to talk to Angel to see if they could get put on. They weren't getting anywhere selling weed, and they felt they were ready for bigger and better things. I took their numbers, usually made them wait a day or so before calling, then gave instructions on where they could pick up their package, what time, and who to give the money to.

Next Kids was directly across the hall and since it was a smaller store, only one person needed to be over there to work. I brought Danielle in to help me out because I didn't trust the other girls that worked in the store. Over the past couple of weeks she had proven her loyalty not only to Keyshia, but to me as well and that meant a lot.

She would come into the store carrying a different book bag each time and wait for the buyer. To avoid suspicion she always made huge purchases to make it appear as if she was a regular customer.

Now mind you, my locations weren't always the same. I knew better than to fall into a routine and I knew more than enough people that worked throughout the mall so I would switch up the drop off's and what not between stores.

Sometimes I would arrange for Caleb to meet me during lunch or after work, and he would have one of his lackeys drive up here and they would do the hand off in the parking lot. This was also primetime for me to give him the money I had on me.

I even got more creative, I had Caleb or Danielle meet someone at the Magic Johnson Theater and put it under the seat. Shit was genius, you could go watch a movie, and literally leave with a coke and a smile.

Angel had been right, with the correct players and pieces in place, it was easy. It was almost like everyone knew what was going on so to question the obvious would be stupid. Everyone knew who my brother was as well as who I had behind me so I didn't have to worry about anyone trying to strong arm me. Security wasn't a problem because the mall didn't have any and there weren't any cameras in the store so I was good.

I got paid $8.50 to work at Next, after eight hours a day, and forty hours a week that's what; $680.00 before taxes? I was going home with five grand easy on top of what the government was taking off the top from me.

So just like that, I was a drug dealer and like DMX said in Belly; "Ain't no money, like dope money".

Chapter Twenty-Three

Up until an hour ago, I hadn't spoken to nor had I seen CJ since our little incident at the abortion clinic. Yes he wanted me to terminate my pregnancy, yes he was upset when I told him I was keeping the baby, and yes I still wanted to punch him in the face but I decided to be the bigger person and invite him to come to the doctor with me.

So here we sat.

What I wasn't going to do was tell him that I thought he smelt good, that I liked the way his Polo sweater seemed to fit him just right, that I had thought about kissing him, or that when we hugged my little lady began to pulsate. That I wouldn't do.

I admit, I did miss him, but no matter how cute he was, he had played me for the last time and I wasn't about to be his fool anymore. I would be cordial with him because he was the father of my child, but we would never be on some relationship shit ever again.

"Asjiah Cappelli?"

For a second, I thought Mary Poppins was going to be standing in the doorway but instead she was replaced with a forty something year old black woman who actually looked happy to see me.

CJ held the door as we followed the nurse into the hallway.

After weighing me, and taking my blood pressure, she led us to the ultrasound room.

"Dr. Shah will be in to see you shortly."

I was reluctant for her to leave because I didn't want to be left alone with him.

"Aren't you supposed to undress or something?"

STRIPPING ASJIAH

"You would like that wouldn't you?"

"Do you always have to be so mean A'?"

"I'm playing boy be quiet. But no, I don't have to undress this time. They just need to run this wand across my stomach so we can see the baby, listen to the heart beat and make sure everything is developing properly.

"Have you thought of names?"

I climbed up onto the table and pondered my answer for a second. "Not really, I've just been calling it baby Jai."

"I like that."

"Really? I mean we can change it to something else if you want."

"Nah, that's fine for now, we can always think of something else later."

He looked nervous, like he wanted to say something but wasn't sure on how to form his sentence so it would come out right.

"Asjiah I…"

I was thankful when she tapped on the door because I wasn't in the mood for his apologies and judging by the start of that sentence, he was about to give me one of his "Asjiah I shouldn't have" speeches.

"Hello Asjiah, how are you doing today?"

Dr. Shah was this beautiful Indian woman that couldn't have been any older than thirty-two. Her skin was bronzed and flawless and she had jet black hair that was pulled back into a clip.

"I'm fine."

"And who is this handsome young man?" She smiled at CJ and waited for their introduction.

"This is Christian."

BY SA'RESE

"Are you the baby's father?"

CJ extended his hand and gave a picture perfect smile, "Yes ma'am, nice to meet you."

"And you as well. Now, let's get started shall we?"

I scooted back on the table and rested my head on the pillow while she unzipped my hoodie and lifted my t-shirt.

"No stretch marks, how impressive."

"What's that?" CJ gestured towards the gel that she was spreading over my stomach.

"This is to help the probe glide gently across her abdomen.

"Does it hurt?"

I was surprised that he was asking so many questions and getting so involved. Given he didn't want the baby in the first place; it was a little weird to see him show so much interest.

"No, it doesn't hurt at all."

He stepped closer to the bed and began playing in my hair as we watched the little figure on the screen come to life.

"The heart beat is nice and strong; everything looks good, nice and healthy."

I looked at CJ whose eyes displayed a child like look of excitement.

We both seemed to be caught up in the moment, marveling at the screen watching this little person that we created.

"Well that's a hand, there's a head, a little bottom, two feet and..."

You would've thought we were waiting for our winning lottery numbers to be called the way we were hanging on her every word. I was anxious to hear what I was having although I had already lied and told him it was a boy.

"That right there; is his little pee-pee."

STRIPPING ASJIAH

CJ kissed my hand and then my forehead as he beamed with joy. I was having a boy, my little boy. I was right after all.

"Let's see if we can get him to move a little bit."

She gently pressed the sides of my stomach and magically it looked as if he began to dance. His tiny hands waved to us and I began to cry as I thought of how close I had come to killing him.

Dr. Shah cleaned my stomach and left the room promising to bring us pictures of our son when she returned.

After struggling with the stupid paper covering they placed on the table, I managed to sit up. I mumbled curse words, almost zipping my hair up in my sweatshirt.

Thanks to the prenatal vitamins I had been taking, it was out of control. I kept it coiled in a bun or wore it curly most of the time because it was too long to for me to wear straight.

"I can't believe it A', you're carrying my son." CJ placed his hands around my belly.

"I know right." I guided him to the spot where the baby was resting and momentarily lost myself in his smile as he felt him kick.

"That's my little man."

"Alright, here you are." Dr. Shah reentered the room carrying black and white photos of the ultrasound.

"Thank you."

"Of course; take care of her, and I'll see you again in a few weeks."

CJ sat next to me as we looked over the pictures together. I couldn't believe that we were going to be parents. A decision not to use a condom led to a plus sign on a pregnancy test and now we were looking at our baby.

"Asjiah listen, I'm so sorry for putting you through all of this, but I really want to be there; for you, and for our baby."

BY SA'RESE

He tilted my chin like he usually did when he was getting ready to kiss me and stared into my eyes. "I love you A'."

I turned my head just as our lips were about to touch.

"CJ I can't." I hopped down, grabbed my purse and opened the door.

"At least let me take you to dinner."

Why was he making this so hard for me? Wasn't it enough that I had let him accompany me to the doctor? Just because he suddenly had a change of heart and wanted to be father of the year, was that supposed to erase taking me to the meat market? Was his smile supposed to be enough to wipe away the image in my mind of him fucking Corey?

I just wanted to go home, to go back to Grandma-me's and go to bed, but he had to entice me with food.

"Fine, but I'm driving my own car."

"You really are cute pregnant."

"Shut up."

10.25.2000

I told him.

At Olive Garden over dinner, I told him.

He was having an "I'm going to be a father" rant when I just wanted to enjoy my chicken scampi, salad and breadsticks but he just kept talking. He wanted me to name the baby after him. He wanted to go to all my doctor's appointments; which was fine, but then he suggested that we move in together and that's when I couldn't take anymore so I told him.

I told him that Cash was still alive. I told him that I heard him upstairs, that he had touched my panties, I described my room, and when his eyes began to squint at the corners like they normally do when he's upset, I told him that I had packed up all my things and went to Grandma-me's house.

He insisted that I come home with him, or that he move over there with me but of course I said no.

1. I didn't want to live in his house, or sleep in his bed, a bed that I now know him and Corey had sex in several times, and 2. Grandma-me didn't know him, nor do I want him to come over there and disrupt the little bit of peace that I had. I told him just like I told Angel; I don't need a fucking babysitter.

Besides, it was Donte and Mike that cleaned up after the mess I made, all he did was sit in the car and wait, so what the hell was he gonna do if Cash did show up again? I'm cool; I'll take my chances on my own.

So yes, I am having a little boy.

I wonder what he'll look like, if he'll have my eyes, my hair, CJ's smile; four months down and five more to go. I can't wait to meet him. Grandma-me said that I could turn the other bedroom into a nursery and that she would go with me to help pick out things for his room. Don't get me wrong, I appreciate all her help, and it's really cute to see her so excited about me having a baby, but I wish it was my mother that was sharing this experience with me instead.

She will never get the chance to see him, to hold her grandson, and he will never get the chance to fall asleep in her arms, to listen to her voice, to smell the sweet scent of jasmine and lavender; crazy that I still remember her scent.

I can't bring her back, no matter how hard I try, no matter how much I wish my tears will raise her from her grave. All I

BY SA'RESE

can do is tell stories, show him pictures (the few that I do have), and take him to visit her at the cemetery. He needs to know how special she was, and still is to me.

Baby Jai didn't need to know that his daddy couldn't keep his dick in his pants nor that he didn't want him, all of that didn't matter now. I guess it takes some of us longer than others to come to grips with our responsibilities and now that he has, I can honestly say that he's trying so I will give him a chance.

I never agreed with girls who purposely kept their child from seeing its father or depriving him of having any involvement in their lives just because the relationship didn't work out and they were bitter. I didn't want to be that girl and although Sean turned out to be a murderer, he was a very important part of my life for eight years in which he was a great father. My reasons for not liking CJ had nothing to do with our child so I had to put my feelings to the side and associate with him based on our son. All I wanted was for the both of us to raise a happy baby boy and to give him all the things that we missed out on as kids. Who knows, in time maybe we could discuss getting back together but right now the only thing that mattered was our child.

STRIPPING ASJIAH

Chapter Twenty-Four

The air blew tender kisses against her damp skin causing dew-like drops to form along the small of her back. She shivered slightly as she massaged shea butter across her chest causing her nipples to harden against her touch.

As the familiar sensation of arousal knocked on the door between her legs she yearned for someone to answer. It had been far too long since she had felt a man's touch; too many nights had passed since she had a hard, attractive body pressed against hers. Thrusting, pumping, breathing heavily in her ear; she wanted to be reminded of what that moment felt like when your legs began to shake, your eyes close slightly and roll in the back of your head, and suddenly, you begin to climax.

She wanted to feel sexy again and since her release, she had felt anything but; sure her scars had healed and her body was back to normal, but being in that hospital had stripped her of her confidence, the bandages had been taken off but in their place were insecurities.

Camouflaging her outside appearance was easy but there wasn't any makeup she could put on to disguise the fears that had been embedded in her heart. That fuckin' junkie had almost killed her left her for dead; the image of his face, those eyes that scar, would forever be etched in her mind.

The wind gently pushed the curtains apart allowing her the chance to momentarily bathe in the sunlight.

"I think you're beautiful."

Startled, Keyshia placed one hand over her breast and the other over her vagina in an attempt to cover herself from Danielle's eyes.

"How long have you been standing there?"

"Long enough," Danielle walked into the room stopping once she was directly in front of her.

"You don't have to hide."

She began to trace the outline of her nude body stopping once she got to the scar on her face, she studied the stitches as if Keyshia was a neglected baby doll that had been carefully sewn back together.

Their lips were so close, one waiting for the other to make the first move.

Inhibitions gave way to carnal desires as the curiosity that had once lain dormant began to overflow and rise to the surface as they started to kiss. The touch, her scent, Danielle's skin against hers; the sensation was like nothing else she had experienced.

Keyshia's mind raced as she fought with herself mentally asking if this was appropriate, if her feeling turned on by another woman was okay. Her conscience left the room as she removed Danielle's shirt, unclasped her bra and suckled her breast. The cry of ecstasy that escaped her lips caused her to nurse her engorged nipples even more.

Danielle removed herself from Keyshia's lips and pushed her down on the bed.

"Spread your legs."

Apprehension made her heart skip, embarrassment made her face flush, but lust made her bite her bottom lip and do as Danielle requested.

Danielle could tell that this was her first experience with a girl so she had to be careful not to take her over the edge too soon. She started by nibbling on the inside of her thighs, kissing her mound, then she began to lick inside of her hole and on her lips. Her tongue teased her clit causing the inexperienced virgin to arch her back and attempt to escape.

"Don't move." Danielle placed her hands underneath her butt holding her in place this time using her fingers simultaneously while she sucked enthusiastically on her pearl.

"Mmm…"

"You like that?"

Keyshia could barely speak as she tried to comprehend the way Danielle was making her feel. She had gotten head plenty of times but not like this, with a girl it was much more intimate, it was as if she knew her body better than she did.

"Yesss…"

Their bodies interlocked like puzzle pieces as Danielle turned around and positioned herself in a way that would allow both of them to receive oral pleasure.

There was no longer time for reasoning or justification; vanilla and oatmeal exploded on Keyshia's palette as she plunged her tongue inside of Danielle's walls. She used her thumb to massage her g-spot applying just the right amount of pressure.

"Ooh right there baby, right there."

Danielle moved her fingers in a rapid left and right movement across Keyshia's clit.

"Cum with me mami…shit….mmm…"

"Ahh,"

She sat up and wiped the corners of her mouth as she watched her cream drip down Keyshia's chin. Danielle's fingertips did figure eights in Keyshia's fountain splashing in its puddles.

"Turn over."

Unaware of what was in store for her next; once again she complied and did as she was told.

An iridescent pink caught a ray of sunlight which made it glimmer even more. Danielle twirled the 8inch dildo around in her mouth and giggled.

Keyshia had done a lot of kinky shit before her accident but this was by far the wildest. If she let her put that inside of her, would that make her a lesbian? Or had she already crossed that threshold when she was eating her pussy? Either way she was turned on and plastic or not, this was the closest a dick had been to her in a couple months and she planned on taking it.

The toy penis filled her up creating an overwhelming pulsing inside of her as Danielle activated the vibrator. She moved her hand in a clockwise motion in and out, slow then fast, fast then slow.

The girls were so caught up in each other that they didn't hear the keys in the door, they were deaf to the footsteps that trailed through the kitchen and down the hallway until it stopped in front of the bedroom door.

"Shit," Groping his dick he instantly got hard looking at the two women make love to each other on the bed.

"Y'all couldn't wait for me?"

The sound of his voice made her smile as she turned around to face him.

"Mike!"

"Mike?"

Caught off guard, Danielle looked from her man then back to Keyshia.

"Y'all know each other?"

STRIPPING ASJIAH

Chapter Twenty-Five

Danielle's sweet, seductive like persona was now replaced with an accusatory tone.

"Answer me Mike; how the fuck do you know her?"

"Calm down babe, it's not what you think."

"Oh really, so you want me to believe that she's just some casual acquaintance of yours?"

Keyshia was still sitting on the bed trying to get a handle on her thoughts. The sudden appearance of Mike also brought memories of her past.

The last time she saw him she was face down ass up allowing him to pummel her anally. She had done things with him she hadn't done with anyone else, she let him videotape them having sex and now she was in his house, their house, making lesbian love to his girlfriend.

Everything began to flood back into her mind at blinding speeds. She remembered Danielle telling her that she had been staying at the hotel with her boyfriend the same night that she found her; so this is who she had been talking about. She began to wonder if Danielle had known about her all along, possibly been shown the footage of her sucking her man's dick as if her life depended on it. What if the only reason she invited her to stay in her home was so that she could extract revenge on the slut who had slept with her boyfriend.

"I think I should go." Keyshia scrambled around the room trying to gather her things so that she could leave.

"Pon tu el culo," Danielle began to speak in a mixture of Spanish and English as her temper escalated. "You aren't going anywhere!"

Mike approached Danielle attempting to kiss her which only seemed to upset her further.

"Don't be like that babe, look, it only happened once and it didn't mean anything. We were just having fun."

"You said that you wouldn't have sex with another girl unless we did it together." Her voice soon turned to a child like pout as Mike began fingering her. She started unfastening his jeans whispering something in his ear causing their attention to turn back to their voyeur.

"I'm sorry, it was last summer and I never would've agreed to stay here if I knew that…."

Danielle held out her hand and motioned for Keyshia to come back to the bed. She placed her index finger over her lips silencing her apologies.

"It's okay."

Still naked, she began to fondle Keyshia's exposed breast while biting gently on her neck.

Before undressing, Mike reached into his bag and pulled out a baggie containing a variety of different colored tablets.

"Keep going."

Danielle eased a frightened looking Keyshia onto the bed picking up where she had left off before Mike interrupted them.

"What are you doing?"

"Shhh," Danielle leaned back against Mike gripping the back of his neck as he kissed her and placed one of the pills on her tongue. Continuing the exchange, she then did the same thing to Keyshia.

"Swallow it. Trust me, it makes the sex better."

Keyshia's mind was doing summersaults, too many things were happening at once. A part of her wanted to grab her clothes and run out of here as fast as she could but the other side of her was intrigued, enticed by the moment, turned on by the way Danielle touched her, the way she talked to her, her pussy began to throb while she watched Mike stroke his erection.

"It's only ecstasy, you'll be fine."

Before she could protest or show any signs of resistance, he was in between her legs and Danielle was straddling her face.

Her body was on fire, everything they did to her made her skin feel like small electrical currents were passing through it.

After he came, Mike pulled out of her and bent Danielle over placing his hand around her neck while he fucked her ferociously from behind.

"Ooh, like that baby, just like that. Fuck me. Fuck me harder baby, harder."

Keyshia reached down and began stimulating her clit while she kissed her.

"Mmmm, let me taste that pussy."

Keyshia pulled Danielle's hair forcing her head down crying out in pleasure as she ate her out.

So many different positions, sex that seemed to go on forever, she had never participated in anything like this. Was she gay, was she straight, did this threesome make her bisexual? She wasn't sure what she was but she did know that after today, she would never have sex with just men ever again.

BY SA'RESE

Chapter Twenty-Six

"But I wanna go with you."

"I have a busy day munchkin. Going to the park will be much more fun than sitting in my office by yourself all day."

"I don't wanna go to the park, and I wouldn't be by myself. I can play with Ms. Theresa and we can go down to the beach and collect sea shells, or make sandcastles, I promise I won't go in the water. Please?"

The little girl's nose turned red, her cheeks rosy as she struggled to find the right words to say. Tears began to form in her eyes appearing as if the sky would open up and it would begin to rain any minute.

"Don't cry." She gently placed her hand against her face and wiped her sadness away.

"Be a good girl and go with Ms. Carmen, once you get to the park you'll forget all about me. The sooner I go to work, the sooner I can come back home.

"Come on! Stop being a crybaby and let's go!" Her brother's impatience was dangling from the backseat window.

"Smile for me baby doll and I'll bring you cupcakes later."

The promise of sweets made the taste of her defeat a little easier to swallow. She still didn't want to go to the park but her mother wasn't budging so she did as she was told flashing deep dimples.

"I love you."

"I love you too."

She laughed and made silly faces at her mom as she watched her pull into the garage.

STRIPPING ASJIAH

Excitement bubbled over as she raced down the stairs and waited for her to exit the car. The door opened and blood covered her feet.

"Help me."

Her tiny hands began to search her body, feeling across her stomach, her chest, and her arms.

"I'll make it stop mommy, I'll make it stop."

As soon as she would find one hole, another would appear. Her mother began to cry. Helpless, their sobs merged together. She kept bleeding, but how, from where? There was so much blood.

"What are you doing?"

"Daddy, its mommy, help her, you have to help her!"

Confusion cloaked the child's face as her father picked her up and took her away from the lifeless figure she was so desperately clinging to.

"No! No! You can't leave her there, you have to save her!" Kicking and screaming she fought, tried to get away, she wanted to go back to the car and be with her, wanted to do as she had been taught in school, as her parents had taught her and call 911. She wanted to save her, she had to save her.

Blood stained her face as she wiped her eyes, she thought he was carrying her to the stairs to get her out of the sea of blood that had become the garage floor but he didn't put her down, he didn't tell her it would be okay as he ran back and attempted to save his wife; instead he took her into the house, closed the door and left Jai to die.

"No!"

"Ssh, it's okay Asjiah, it's going to be okay."

BY SA'RESE

I was screaming. My hair was clinging to my forehead, my t-shirt damp, heart racing. I couldn't breathe, my lungs were on fire, and my throat was dry.

"He killed her."

I continued to cry as Grandma-me tried her best to comfort me. I threw the covers off my bed onto the floor, touched my body, and looked at my hands out of fear that everything would be drenched in blood.

"You're okay Asjiah, sssh, you're okay."

I felt sick. Often I would be plagued with nightmares; each dream different but the outcome was still the same. I got to witness her die all over again, and no matter what I did, no matter how hard I tried, I was never able to save her.

The clock read 5:45 am, the exact time I was born yet as Grandma-me rocked me and smoothed my hair I felt like I was dying.

"Yo, I just seen dude, he said its all clear, let's go."

Angel tucked the shank he had spent all day carving into his back pocket and left the cell.

Him and Gabe had been watching, planning, waiting on the opportune moment to strike and it had finally come.

Amazing the things you can get a corrections officer to do for a little bit of money. Hell, it was hard to find someone who wasn't corrupt in the prison system. You just had to know who was who and how to exploit their greed in order to use it to your advantage.

In Angel's case it was easy. A lot of the guards knew who he was on the outside or they had worked in the same prisons that his uncle's had been housed in previously.

STRIPPING ASJIAH

However, this time he had Gabrielle to thank. The C.O. that was helping them out in this particular situation, just so happened to be the father of his older sister's kids. They ran into each other during recreation, exchanged a few words and everything else was history. The guard was able to tell him what times he ate, when he went out to the yard and what times he was most likely to be in his house.

His cellmate had been released a few days ago on good behavior so for the time being, he would be by himself until they brought in some other child molester, or drug dealer to keep him company.

Gabe tried to contain his excitement as they weaved their way through the other inmates, down the stairs, across the hall and to the other side of the pod. At first he was worried that his friend was going to let the boy go, allow him to get away with attempted robbery, murder and busting down his girl but then Angel began to talk. There were brief windows when he displayed vulnerability, pain, betrayal, and other times where there were signs of anger, disgust and hate for those who had wronged him.

He painted a very sordid picture, explained how their upcoming acts would affect each person involved, some of which made him second guess what he was doing. But he was in too deep now, they were steps away from their destination and there was no turning back.

They stood in silence at first, watching him as he did sit ups with his back facing them. Ignorant to what was about to happen.

Angel casually walked into the cell and sat on the bottom bunk.

He had practically been handed to them gift wrapped with a pretty little bow on top.

BY SA'RESE

Before LT realized what was going on the order had already been given.

"Grab him and shut the door."

"Go slow."

The intoxicated brunette turned her back and seductively draped her blouse over her shoulder. The alcohol cursing through her system gave her the extra confidence she needed as she continued to strip to the music.

He watched her body coil and wind in snake like movements as her clothes disappeared layer by layer. In a way she reminded him of her. A milky white complexion, long hair, full breasts, a petite frame; but something was off. He tilted his beer bottle to her as approval that he liked what she was doing and as she stood before him naked it came to him.

"Put these on."

Smiling, the girl took a sip of her drink and continued to dance.

"You just told me to take my clothes off, now you want me to put them back on?"

"Not all of them, just these." Cash dangled a pair of black cheeky boy shorts and waited for her to take them.

"I just want to see how they look on you before I take them back off."

"Hey, are these someone else's panties? Where is the tag?"

"Don't worry about all that; just put them on."

"I'm not a medium, I'm an extra small." She stumbled over to the bathroom positioning herself in front of the mirror so she could see her backside.

"They are kinda cute huh?"

STRIPPING ASJIAH

Cash kissed the back of her neck, and palmed her ass lifting her onto the vanity. She giggled girlishly as he pushed the crotch of the fragile cotton to the side and inserted his fingers inside of her.

"Be a good girl and spread your legs for me Asjiah."

"Mmmm, my name's not Asjiah its Jessica."

He let his jeans fall around his ankles, exposing himself.

With eyes heavy from the liquor she had been drinking Jessica glanced down at his semi hard penis and laughed.

"You need some help baby?" Slithering down from the counter she got on her knees and began her attempt to further arouse him.

"I knew you wanted this dick Asjiah."

"That's not my name."

Grabbing her by the wrists Cash forcefully turned the girl around bending her over the sink.

"Stop it, you're hurting me!" Jessica immediately began to sober up as her attacker tried to force himself inside of her.

"C'mon, don't fight me baby girl, give that pink pussy to Uncle Cash."

Shoving him with all her might, she pushed past him and gathered her clothes off the floor as fast as she could.

"You're fucking sick. I'm getting out of here."

Cash sat down at the table as she stormed out of the room. Snorting the remaining lines of coke he waited for the narcotic to take over his senses. This was getting out of control. He needed to find her, to be with her, he was running out of patience, getting tired of pretending these random girls were her hoping it would momentarily satisfy his cravings.

He walked over to the dimly lit closet, undressed and entered his sanctuary.

BY SA'RESE

Photos of Asjiah when she was a little girl, pictures that he had taken from his mother's house, vulnerable images he had captured while he watched her all hung on the wall. The laundry he had taken from her room, this was the one place he could go when he wanted to feel her, to smell her.

He smiled as he toyed with the rope and the duck tape that lay on the shelf. He laughed haphazardly as he picked up the gag and the handcuffs; he traced her lips on one of the photographs before kissing it.

Revenge was going to be so sweet.

LT was baffled; after everything that happened last summer he knew for sure Angel would kill him. But here he sat across from him in his cell being given the opportunity to walk out scot free.

Angel told him that Gabrielle knew someone in the DA's office that could take a second look at his case, file an appeal and within a few months, he could be going home.

He told him that Caleb would link up with him to put him onto what was going on in the streets and all he had to do was send him a couple of dollars to put on his books.

Was it really that easy?

He didn't know the length of Angel's bid but maybe he had come to terms with the amount of time him and Gabe would be spending in here and as a result he knew he needed to mend fences and hand everything over to him.

With Angel out of the way that would eliminate the competition and more importantly, that would leave him with Stacey. He would say yes and agree to his requests but little did Angel know; he had a plan of his own. He would walk out of here once released, and never look back. By the time Angel came home, he would find that there was no stash of money waiting for him, nor would Stacey be there to greet him with her legs wide open, they would both be long gone, somewhere far away with both his paper, and his drugs.

"So what's it gonna be? Can you do that for me?"

Gabe stood by the door keeping a watch out the tiny window making sure things were still on the up and up.

LT attempted to slow his breathing and keep his voice from shaking. He didn't want to seem too geeked.

"Yeah, I can handle that for you."

"Good, good, that's just what I wanted to hear."

In an instant Gabe was behind LT pushing him up against the side of the bed. He used the sheets they had knotted together to bind around his waist and tie him to the bed post.

"What the fuck is going on?"

Angel retrieved the shank that was in his back pocket and dangled it out in front of him.

"You're not scared now are you?"

Before he could answer Gabrielle shoved a pair of socks in his mouth preventing him from making any noise.

"I told you I was going to let you out of here, what I didn't say was that it was going to be in one piece."

Gabe held out one of LT's hands struggling with him momentarily in order to get him to straighten his fingers.

Angel smiled as he approached his cousin, "Now I'll be honest, this may hurt a little bit."

Chapter Twenty-Seven

Halloween, the day of the dead; a night dedicated to all things evil, devils, ghouls, goblins, witches, vampires, and werewolves alike. I chose not to dress up. I figured being myself was scary enough.

I told Marie that I would take the kids trick or treating so here I was, in the living room in front of the mirror putting the finishing touches on their costumes.

"You put makeup on too Aja?"

I had painted all of them up to resemble zombies each with different special effects. I wanted to recreate what my mother used to do for us, well Angel at least because I always had to be the cute stuff; Carebears, smurfs, snorks. I remember being so fascinated with the way she would transform him just from using a $5.00 paint kit she had gotten from the store.

I wasn't as good as she was but I had managed to make Hope look like she was crying blood, Dorian's neck was tore open, James heart had been ripped out and Tiffany was missing half of her scalp.

"I don't want to wear it, this is for you guys."

"Pwease?"

I had to laugh at her mispronunciation of the word please and once the other kids began to chime in asking me to do it I gave in.

"Okay, okay, but not a lot."

I darkened the rims of my eyes using a charcoal eyeliner pencil, and a mixture of some of the black paint from the kit. I put drops of red at the corners of my mouth and drew two bite marks on the side of my throat.

"You look like a vampire Asjiah!" Dorian stood behind me in the mirror smiling at my quick make up job. I had straightened my hair the night before so along with the length, the black eyeliner and the color of my eyes, he was right, I did look like the undead. Along with the black sweater I had on, distressed jeans and black knee high boots, I looked pretty gothic.

"Look at all my little monsters," Marie stood in the doorway glancing over all of us. "Asjiah y'all be safe out there."

"Alright, come on everybody."

A perfect full moon and a sky full of stars greeted us as we stepped out into the warm autumn night. Kids were running up and down the street scurrying from house to house trying to beat each other to doorsteps that promised tricks or treats.

"Everybody hold hands, if y'all start acting crazy or try to leave each other we will turn around and go back home, understand?"

"Yes." They linked hands and made sure their shoes were tied before descending the stairs.

"Boo!"

Startled, the kids screamed and ran back up the steps hiding behind me for protection.

I laughed as CJ pulled off the ridiculous mask he was wearing.

"It's just me, I'm sorry."

Realizing it wasn't the boogeyman they settled down and picked up their pumpkin baskets.

"What's up A'?"

I let him kiss me on the cheek while we hugged. I had to brush off his advance to put his hand on my stomach because I didn't know if Marie was watching.

After our interaction at the doctor's office and over dinner CJ had made it a regular habit to call and check on me and the baby everyday, he would ask me if I needed anything or if there was anything he could do for me. He was really trying. He even started shopping for baby Jai. I had several outfits that he had bought, along with a stroller, a pack n' play and other things he couldn't wait to buy.

I invited him to go trick or treating with us because I knew he wanted to spend time with me and also because he insisted. He didn't want me out by myself given the fact that Cash was still on the loose. I tried to assure him that I would be okay especially since I was only taking them around the neighborhood and I was sure Caleb was somewhere watching me but that wasn't reassuring enough.

He did look kinda cute; a grey Abercrombie hoodie, stonewashed jeans and wheat Timberlands, he always could make the simplest outfits look so sexy. Perhaps that's what made it so easy for me to let him hold my hand as we walked behind the kids.

"So how are you?"

"Aside from having to pee every ten minutes, I'm good. Most of my sickness is over with so I can pretty much eat whatever I want to now."

"That's a good thing right?"

"Yeah, throwing up is not fun."

"I see you're getting kind of thick." CJ squeezed my butt and laughed, running ahead a little bit so I couldn't hit him for doing so."

"Ha, ha, you like that don't you?"

"Hell yeah I like it."

STRIPPING ASJIAH

Placing his hands around my waist he turned me towards him.

"Why don't you stay the night with me and I can show you how much I like it."

"CJ…"

I tried to ignore him by keeping my eyes on the kids but he was so close to my ear, right next to one of my spots, he was teasing me, seducing me without trying and he knew it.

I was about to give in to temptation but then I felt something yank on my hair.

"Ouch!"

I grabbed the back of my head and looked in the direction that I had been pulled.

"A', what's wrong? Is it the baby? Are you okay?"

He walked around me looking for signs that weren't there, signals that something was wrong.

"Yeah, I'm fine. It felt like someone pulled my hair."

"You could've snagged it on my sweatshirt."

"I guess so."

He must've seen the worry in my face, the way my eyebrows wrinkled, he pulled me closer to him and hugged me tightly looking in both directions trying to see if there was some invisible assailant that had suddenly vanished.

Tiffany was yawning and Hope's makeup was smeared from her rubbing her eyes. The boys looked worn-out as well and all of their pumpkins were filled to the rim from the treats they had accumulated throughout the night.

CJ picked the girls up while Dorian and James walked a few steps ahead.

I held his hand tightly trying to purge unwanted thoughts out of my brain.

BY SA'RESE

I knew someone had touched me. The tug was too aggressive for it to have been an accident. I felt his hand against my skin. And as we crossed the street and headed back towards Marie's house I swore I saw him, under the shadows of the lamppost watching me.

"If I should die before I wake, I pray the Lord, my soul to take, Amen."

I kissed each of the boys on the cheeks and turned the TV on so they could watch Goosebumps.

Walking down the hall I could hear Tiffany and Hope giggling, I stopped in the doorway where they couldn't see me so I could eavesdrop.

"Nope, no monsters under here," CJ dusted his knees off after looking underneath both of their beds.

"What about in there?" Hope made it sound as if she was saying "near" instead of there as she pointed to the closet.

"Yeah, look in the closet."

I tried not to laugh as CJ walked over to the closet, opened it and pretended as if something had pulled him inside. Both girls snatched their blankets up over their heads peeking from underneath to make sure nothing was going to get them.

"Nope, not in there either."

Watching him interact with them made me think of how he would be with baby Jai. He was really good with the kids and although we had disagreements every now and then, I knew he would be a good father.

"Okay, that's enough, time to go to bed."

"A-ja can we stay up just a little while longer?"

CJ batted his eyelashes and helped the girl's plea for more late night antics, "Yeah A-ja, please?"

Tiffany thought he was the funniest thing in the world. Bursting into hysterics she laughed as he did his best little girl voice.

"Alright, okay. You can watch a movie but that's it."

"Yay!"

CJ helped the girls with their prayers while I put in The Rescuers down Under. I set the timer to automatically turn the TV off then tucked them into bed.

"Goodnight A-ja."

"Goodnight."

"That was really sweet of y'all to take them out tonight. I know they sure do appreciate that." Marie was sitting in her usual spot in the kitchen eating ice cream.

"No problem, we had fun too."

"Is there any mail here for me?" I skimmed through the stack of envelopes above the sink and picked out all the ones with my name on it.

"You two can stay if you want."

"Nah, that's okay. I have to go to work in the morning," I nudged CJ in the arm before he could accept her offer, "And I'm sure Christian has things to do too right?"

"Huh? Oh yeah, right, maybe some other time."

We said our goodbyes and as we stepped out onto the porch I found myself looking for signs of Cash.

"A',"

"Asjiah?"

"What?

"You didn't hear me?"

I shook my head and tried to refocus my thoughts. "I'm sorry, what did you say?"

"I said thank you."

BY SA'RESE

"For what," I leaned against one of the brick pillars and gazed up at the stars.

"For tonight, it was nice. I never thought I'd enjoy trick or treating so much, but being with you, and the kids, it was cool."

This was my CJ, the sweet, caring Christian that I knew. We were able to have a night without any arguing, without any sarcastic comments or attitudes and it took me back to how we used to be. Back to when things were easy, before things got complicated.

"Thank you for coming. I'm sure they enjoyed your company just as much as I did. You know, I watched you with Hope and Tiffany, you're really good with them."

CJ closed the space between us, stood in between my legs and placed his hands on my stomach.

"I hope I'm the same way if not better with our baby."

It was something about the moment, something in his eyes. I didn't wait for him to initiate contact; I grabbed his sweater, pulled him into me and kissed him.

"Asji-"

I smiled, hopped down the stairs and turned around once I got to my car.

"Call me tomorrow?"

CJ was beaming on his drive home. Tonight had been perfect.

Any other time he had been around her she would act uptight or as if being near him irritated her but after the first few doctors appointments she had began to loosen up. And tonight, well tonight reminded him of Miami, tonight reminded him of how they used to be in school, how it was when they first met. Tonight there was laughter, they held hands, kissed.

STRIPPING ASJIAH

She kissed him.

He hadn't touched her lips; felt her since she had gotten pregnant. And all of a sudden she was kissing him, he was holding her, and time stood still.

Was it possible that she had found a way to put the past behind them?

Whatever it was, regardless of how she had reached her decision he planned on doing right by her and his son. He would be there for everything, the delivery, first words, first steps; he was even excited about changing diapers.

Getting out of the car, he approached the side door pausing at the rustling noise he heard in the bushes behind him. At first he thought it was some kind of small animal but then he heard breathing.

He placed his key in the lock just as the intruders shadow caught the light but it was too late. Their arms were already around his throat.

"Did you miss me baby?" Corey laughed as her lips brushed against his neck.

"What the fuck are you doing here?"

"I came to see you of course," She sauntered into the foyer behind him and sat down at the kitchen table. "You've been gone for quite some time now, where have you been all day?"

"With A'," CJ stood against the refrigerator with his head leaning against the freezer. He was anxious to come home and go to bed so he could drift off to sleep and live in the dream of him and Asjiah being a family. However, for the moment, he was staring at Corey who clearly failed to acknowledge that their time together was over.

"So you finally talked her into having an abortion? Is her little bastard dead now?"

BY SA'RESE

"Nah, I didn't talk her into anything, and that little bastard is my son; Asjiah's having my son."

Corey's heart went up in flames as she listened to the admiration in his voice. His eyes were filled with promise and hers with tears.

"How could you do this to me CJ? I loved you, I still love you. You told me we were gonna be together, you told me that you and that bitch were done! That as soon as you got back from Miami, you would tell her it was over! You lied to me!"

"Well, things changed."

She wiped her eyes with the back of her hand and tried to stop herself from crying. "You're gonna want me back Christian. When you're tired of shitty diapers, when you get tired of him crying, when she chooses Similac over semen, you'll want me back."

"Get out Corey."

"When she's too tired to have sex and can't stay awake long enough to suck your dick, you'll want me back!"

Corey got up from her chair and walked towards him. "Asjiah's a girl, playing a grown woman's game. It's not too late to walk away from her. If you want a baby," She rubbed the front of his jeans smiling as she felt him harden, "we can always make one."

"Is that right?" CJ aggressively shoved her against the counter and began kissing her roughly on the lips. "So you want to have my baby Corrine? Is that what you want?"

"Yes."

"What about what I want?"

Unbuckling his belt, Corey tried to free him of his restraints.

"Anything, I'll give you anything baby, just tell me what it is."

"Anything?"

STRIPPING ASJIAH

The intermittent tapping of her button dancing across the floor seemed to heighten their intensity as he ripped open her shirt. He squeezed her breasts one by one biting her nipples until they became hard between his lips.

Corey screamed in delight as he teased her with the tip of his raw penis flirting with the act of entering her.

"Tell me baby, what do you want?"

The warmth of her body was too much to resist as he slid himself inside of her, "I want..." then back out again "you to leave."

"What?" Her eyes were half closed and her body was still in shock as she tried to decipher what was going on.

CJ walked into the bathroom, got a wet wipe for himself then handed one to Corey.

"Here, clean yourself up then get out." Fastening his pants, he patiently waited for her to comply.

"Are you fucking serious right now? This is how you treat me, like I'm some kind of hoe?"

CJ tried not to laugh as he watched her fumble with her clothes. There was no doubt in his mind that he was making the right choice.

She was all for Asjiah having an abortion, now she so willingly offered up her uterus because she thought that it was going to keep him. She didn't really want a child; she wanted whatever would keep him away from Asjiah.

He knew she would be a good mother, after tonight he was certain that whatever problems they had experienced before was over but first he needed to eliminate what had caused all their issues in the first place.

"You're moving too slow."

"Get your fucking hands off of me!" Struggling, Corey snatched away from him as he ushered her towards the door.

"Goodbye Corrine."

"Wait, wait! I know this isn't you talking; you just need time to think things over, you think you need to be with her just because she's having your baby, but you don't, I know you love me Christian."

"Drive safe."

The door closed in her face and the darkness enveloped her. Why was this happening? Why was he turning his back on her after everything they had been through? Corey got in her car and began to drive home but instead of feeling sorry for herself, instead of getting upset, she smiled. She smiled because she suddenly had an epiphany. She knew what she had to do in order to get him back, she knew what she needed to do to make him love her again and the thought of it brought her joy.

STRIPPING ASJIAH

Chapter Twenty-Eight

Snow fell from the sky in delicate flurries that appeared to dance a romantic Waltz with the wind.

I had only seen Keyshia once since her release but that was in passing with a wave and a promise to call each other later. My interaction with Danielle was business oriented so unless she was talking money, we didn't really speak. Factor in me being five months pregnant, going to the doctor, and spending quality time with CJ and Grandma-me, I really didn't have time in my schedule for girls night out.

But today none of that was a problem, CJ was out of town, I had the day off from Next, things were running smoothly on Caleb's end and Grandma-me practically kicked me out so she could make preparations for little pooh.

I wasn't due until April but she had already started preparing the room adjacent to mine. I knew it made her happy so I left her and Bear at home while I went to Danielle's house for dinner.

I rang the bell that corresponded with her apartment then knelt down to wipe a smudge off my wheat Timberlands. I decided to wear grey sweatpants that read Abercrombie across the butt, and a white long sleeved thermal. My hair was in a neat ponytail and aside from the gold cross that adorned my neck, I looked pretty plain.

I allowed my nose to lead me down the hall towards the smell of bananas and fresh peaches.

"What's up?"

There was a faint scar on her face from where the doctor's had given her stitches and had I not seen her in the ICU myself, I wouldn't have known anything happened to her. The weight she had lost while being hooked up to a feeding tube had resurfaced around her waistline and her current weave of choice was a honey blonde, wavy, shoulder length sew in.

"You look amazing."

"And you look like Rudolph."

We laughed as she poked fun at the bright red color of my face caused by the frigid temperatures outside.

After taking my coat off, I hugged her then followed her into the kitchen where Danielle was hard at work. She gave us fried plantains to snack on while she put the finishing touches on dinner which would be Berenjena con Vinagreta.

"Oh my God, you're so cute."

Danielle wiped her hands on the towel that hung over her shoulder then reached out to rub my stomach.

"Mira, the baby kicked!"

Her excitement made me smile. "That's because he smells all this food in here, he's hungry."

"He," Both girls replied in unison and waited for me to confirm.

"Yes, it's a boy."

They fired questions at me about names, colors, clothes, whether or not I would pierce his ear, amongst other things until Danielle realized the stove was still on allowing me to retreat.

"Where's the bathroom?

"Down the hall and to the right, you can use the one in my room."

I wasn't sure how long their arrangement was for but judging from the looks of things Keyshia had gotten pretty comfortable.

I washed my hands and tried to disregard the lubricant and the double sided dildo sitting next to the sink. I guess those weeks spent in the hospital had made her horny and she had resorted to other methods of satisfying herself.

I couldn't knock it because I had never tried it, masturbating that is; I've heard that it's amazing if you know what you're doing, I just never saw the point in putting my fingers somewhere a man could have his tongue or dick. In my opinion, a toy was a poor substitute to a warm, hard body, but hey, to each his own.

If plastic would keep her from backsliding into the bullshit she was on last summer,then she could buy all the fake penis's she wanted. Shit, I'd buy her toys too.

As I walked back into the living room I tried not to pay attention to the way she was standing behind Danielle at the counter; similar to how CJ stands behind me or like one would when they kiss the back of someone's neck. Their mannerisms were too "friendly" too touchy feely, something about them was off.

I took a seat in front of one of the plates Danielle had creatively garnished.

"This is really good, no wonder your hips look like that."

Keyshia affectionately placed her hand over Danielle's, "she keeps me well fed."

There it was again.

I knew I wasn't misreading it that time. Images of the pink dildo flashed in my mind. Were they using that on each other?

I took a few sips of water hoping it would wash away the perverse images but it ended up going down the wrong pipe.

What the fuck was going on here?

"Asjiah are you okay?"

BY SA'RESE

Coughing I nodded my head. I got up from the table and walked around the room holding my arms in the air; someone told me that worked when one was choking.

Just as I thought things couldn't get any weirder I saw his picture.

Picking up the frame I turned back towards the girls.

"Who is this?"

Keyshia chuckled as if I had delivered a punch line for a joke.

Yes, I knew who the boy in the photo was but I wanted to know who he was to Danielle and if Keyshia realized what she had walked into.

"That's my boyfriend Mike."

I looked from Keyshia back to Danielle then back to Keyshia trying to understand what was going on. Was I the only one who thought it ironic to have fucked him last summer, end up with his girlfriend by your bedside, and now you're living in their house? Where the fuck they do that at?

"Keyshia does she know that…"

"Yes."

"So you told her and…"

"Yes."

"Well not exactly." Danielle chimed in grinning at Keyshia while some secret moment passed between them.

My words had become a series of broken sentences, I couldn't figure out what to say or how to say it.

"So…?"

Danielle placed her hand on Keyshia's thigh, "Everybody's cool."

I didn't know what she was implying by "cool" but I wasn't going to inquire any further.

STRIPPING ASJIAH

This was a prime example as to why I didn't venture outside of my bubble. Too much freaky shit happened when I did.

The pain was excruciating, every inch of his body was on fire. He was becoming delirious, mumbling incoherent vulgarities refusing to beg them for mercy.

He was no stranger to pain, he had been shot and stabbed before, but nothing came close to the feeling of having someone dig underneath your fingernails with a piece of sharpened plastic and rip off your nail beds.

For days they tortured him, freely entering his cell as if they shared living quarters. Where were the guards? Why wasn't any one stopping this?

He should've known better than to trust Angel, he should've recognized game and knew that he wouldn't just let him get away after committing such blatant acts of disrespect. But he was too consumed with greed to see that he was bargaining with the devil.

Jealousy had blinded him, enabling him to see only what was in front of him, tunnel vision so to speak; and as the cell began to fade in and out of focus, he prayed for his sight even though that had been taken away the minute Angel cut his eyelids off.

Trapped in an abyss of darkness he was unable to see them as they entered what had become his tomb. Deaths footsteps approached him seductively, stopping within inches of his face sucking his life into its lungs, exhaling the stench of an expired soul into his.

"I loved you, treated you like a little brother," Angel struggled to speak as tears fell from his face.

"I would've done anything for you."

BY SA'RESE

Gabrielle stood in the corner, noiselessly hurting for his friend. He thought about all the things that Angel had told him, the few times that he had opened up and shared memories of his past, the brief glimpses of happiness he allowed him to see. But all of that was overshadowed with the loss of his mother, the absence of his father, the guilt he carried for not being able to keep his sister from being raped, the beatings; he had been through so much at such a young age, it was enough to drive anyone crazy and as he looked into his eyes, it was obvious that he was going mad.

Angel wiped his face and suddenly appeared eerily serene.

"For the past eleven years I've been walking around like a corpse, empty, emotionless, cold but I've finally realized what I'm missing."

The shrill sound of LT's scream reverberated throughout the chamber threatening to break through the fabric that was stuffed in his mouth. Blood gushed from his body covering Angel's hands then dripping onto the floor.

Gabrielle had never feared his friend, but in that horrific moment as he watched him hold his cousins beating heart, for the first time, he was afraid.

STRIPPING ASJIAH

Chapter Twenty-Nine

Danielle and Keyshia had insisted on telling me about their little ménage a trois even though I kindly displayed my disinterest. They sipped Pinot giggling like school girls as they told stories of the pleasures they gave each other while I drank hot chocolate and ate churros.

I was getting sleepy and I wanted nothing more than to go home and get in the bed. Yawning, I stretched lazily and began to gather my things just as the alcohol was festering in Keyshia's blood giving her the courage she needed to say what was on her mind.

"So at what point did you realize your uncle was a rapist? Before or after he had his dick in you?"

"What the fuck did you just say?" I dropped my bag and cocked my head to the right as if that would allow me to hear her better.

Keyshia laughed, took a few swigs from her glass and proceeded to provoke me.

"I'm just saying, maybe if you would've known this nigga was a pedophile before hand I wouldn't have ended up in the hospital."

"Are you really gonna sit here and blame me for what happened to you?"

"I'm not blaming you; I'm telling you that you should apologize."

"Apologize? Are you fucking serious? What the fuck do I have to apologize for? Is it my fault that your crack-headed ass ended up in a hotel with this nigga? Did I tell you to snort coke off this nigga's dick?" Out of habit, I scratched my head like I usually did when confused.

"What do you want me to say? I'm so sorry I wasn't there by your side gobbling dick or to help you shop for Monistat 7 because your hot ass pussy was itching."

"Fuck you Asjiah."

"Nah, hold up, you wanted me to say sorry, so that's what I'm doing. I truly apologize for not being super geeked up to get on all fours and pose cheek to cheek with you while some nigga lubed up my asshole."

Keyshia was in my face before Danielle could get to her.

"Don't get yo' ass whooped Asjiah! Everybody else might be scared of you, but I'm not!"

"Aww," I put my hand to her cheek and faked concern. "Did I hit a nerve? Is your booty still a little sore?" I couldn't help but laugh as I reached around and tapped her playfully on the butt.

"Bitch,"

I grabbed her by the wrist before her hand could connect with my face, squeezed it roughly, and then shoved her down on the couch.

"I don't have time for this shit." Grabbing my purse I walked towards the door.

"Asjiah wait," Danielle shook her head at an intoxicated Keyshia and rushed after me.

"Let her leave! That's her fucking problem; she's used to people chasing after her."

Keyshia picked up her glass and guzzled down the remainder of her wine.

"She's used to people kissing her ass, treating her like she's some kind of goddamn princess or some shit."

"Shut the fuck up!"

STRIPPING ASJIAH

"Make me bitch! Make me!" She wobbled slightly then fell onto the floor.

"Maybe that's why you're so fucked up in the head; your father carved your mother up like a fucking turkey and your uncle is a rapist. What other psychopaths are in your family tree?"

I didn't even think; I just reacted. I may have blacked out; all I remember is taking off towards the living room, and kicking her in the face. I was about to do it again until Danielle pulled me back into the kitchen.

"Mira, calm down, remember the baby."

I looked into her big, doe like eyes and tried to pull myself together. She was right, I couldn't just hall off and beat her ass the way I wanted to, I was pregnant; I had to protect my son.

"She's just upset Asjiah, she feels like you abandoned her."

"I abandoned her?" I tilted my head to the right and arched my left eyebrow. "Whatever. Keyshia and I both know what went down last summer so if she wants to blame me for her poor choices, so be it. She's not woman enough to own up to her own shit so she has to point fingers at someone else. Typical."

I ducked down just as she hurled the wine glass towards the door. It missed Danielle's head by inches and shattered against the wall.

"Put your hands on me again bitch and I'ma fuck you up!" Keyshia wiped blood from her lip and attempted to steady herself against the counter.

"Oh hell no,"

Danielle gently placed her arms around me and pushed me into the hallway, "Calm down, she's drunk. Just ignore her."

I wanted to go back in the house and mush her face into the wall but I had to think about baby Jai. He wasn't used to this, all this drama was making my heart race and I didn't want to do anything to cause him any distress.

"I need my purse."

Danielle cracked the door open and picked my Chanel bag up off the floor.

"I'm so sorry for all of this. I didn't know she was going to act this way."

"Don't apologize for her sloppy ass! What you should do is put her out your house."

Disregarding my last comment, she tried to get me to change my mind about leaving. "Are you sure you don't want to stay?"

"And talk to her when she's like that? Nah, I'm good. If I stay, more then glass is gonna get broke." I tapped on the down button and impatiently waited for the elevator.

"She just needs some time Asjiah."

"She's wasted enough of my time today. Keyshia wants someone to coddle her and I'm not on it. We can clean her up and put Band-Aids on her boo boo's but she ain't gonna do shit but pick the scabs and make them bleed again. I don't know about you, but I'm not doing it anymore."

I felt bad that Danielle had been dragged in the middle of all this but she would learn firsthand that Keyshia cared about no one but herself.

"Thanks for having me over though. You have a really nice place."

My compliment made her smile. She looked a lot better now that she wasn't spending her days in the hospital. Her butterscotch complexion was no longer flushed and the worry that veiled her pretty face was now gone.

"You're welcome. You can come through whenever."

"Thanks, but I doubt I'll be visiting while she's here."

STRIPPING ASJIAH

The elevator doors opened and I could hear Keyshia yelling incoherently from the apartment.

"Look, the two of you made it clear that y'all are involved with each other now, but if you were smart, you'd end it. She's a leech and if you let her, she'll suck the fucking life out of you."

The doors closed and I began my decent back to the lobby. I should've known Keyshia would be on some bullshit. I don't know why I thought we would be able to sit down and talk like civilized adults.

I thought being near death would clear her head, I thought her experience with Cash would've knocked some sense into her; literally, but I guess not.

God had given her a second chance, a get out of hell free card and instead she threw it back in his face, chose not to pass go, and not collect two hundred dollars.

I was still fuming when the bell sounded and the doors to the elevator opened. I was fumbling around in my purse trying to find my car keys, I wasn't paying attention. I allowed my fight with Keyshia to distract me from my surroundings and that's why I didn't see her.

I didn't have enough time to regain my balance when she pushed me, my back slammed against the railing sending agonizing volts of pain through my back.

Suddenly she was on top of me, we exchanged blows and this animalistic instinct kicked in. I wasn't fighting for myself; I was fighting her to protect my child. I balled up and tried to protect my stomach. The look in her eyes told me that this wasn't about her catty dislike for me; she had found a better target. She was trying to kill my baby.

BY SA'RESE

I felt like I was having contractions, the next stronger than the first, each limiting my movements, I felt wet, like I was bleeding but I kept fighting. I had to keep fighting.

The doors opened again and she ran, like a fucking coward.

I scrambled around for my phone; blood covered the screen as I tried to put it to my face.

"Yo,"

"…help me…"

The sound of her voice made his heart stop. Panic set in and he automatically thought the worst as he listened to her plea.

"I didn't… know who else to call."

"Asjiah, A' where are you? Can you tell me where you are?"

"Southgate Towers," The signal dropped and tears flooded my eyes as I placed my hands on my abdomen.

I fainted just as Danielle was running down the hall with my keys in her hand.

"Push Asjiah, you have to push sweetie."

I took a deep breath and did what the doctor instructed.

"One more and it'll all be over."

In an instant they had him wrapped up and under a light, I couldn't tell what was going on but I knew enough to know that he was supposed to be crying.

"Why isn't he crying? Why isn't my baby crying?"

"Shh, it's okay A', its going to be okay."

He was trying to soothe me, wiping sweat off my forehead, moving my hair out of my face, holding my hand. All I wanted was to know why my baby wasn't making any noise.

They put their heads down and said something I couldn't quite make out, then one of them approached me.

"Would you like to hold him?"

STRIPPING ASJIAH

Unaware, I smiled and extended my arms. He was bundled tightly in a blue blanket, hair jet black and curly just like mine, I held him tightly, positioning him close to my heart waiting for him to open his eyes. Eyes that I hoped were the same shade as mine but I never got the chance to see them. I kissed him on his cheeks, whispered loving words into his tiny little ears, held his small hand in mine and that's when I realized how cold he was. That's when I noticed he wasn't moving, when I took in all the faces around me and death spoke in a voice that I had become all too familiar with.

"We're so sorry. He can stay in here for a little while but then we have to take him away. Someone will come in and discuss funeral arrangements with you..."

I don't remember the rest of her words; everything around me seemed to become white noise. I just remember crying, sobbing uncontrollably, screaming until he couldn't take it anymore and requested that they sedate me.

BY SA'RESE

Chapter Thirty

Stacey was beginning to lose it. Paranoia had become her best friend which was only induced by the weed she was smoking. Everything and everyone was her enemy. She was certain that Angel was out to get her and it was only a matter of time before he achieved his goal.

The hard knock on her front door almost made her jump out of her skin. She cautiously peeked through the blinds only to find the UPS man standing on her porch.

"Can I help you?"

"Delivery for a Stacey Johnson,"

"That's me."

"Sign here, and here."

Closing the door she put the box close to her ear and shook it. The words "il mio amore" were above a P.O Box address that she didn't recognize.

"Do you know what this means?"

"No Miss, sorry I don't, I'm not too good with foreign languages."

The postal worker waited patiently as she picked at the tape anxious to open her surprise.

"Aww, this is so cute."

Inside the box, on top of red and black tissue paper was a card with a little white teddy bear on the front. Maybe she had been forgiven after all; perhaps Asjiah had spoken to him and convinced him to work things out.

Opening the card, she read the inscription inside: "Since you took my heart, I thought it was only fair that I give you his."

STRIPPING ASJIAH

A look of perplexity and repulsion cloaked her face as she removed the tissue paper and saw the contents of the box.

The UPS guy closed the space between them and in a quick movement stabbed her in the lower torso, twisting then dragging the box cutter out horizontally.

"Angel say's hello."

Chapter Thirty-One

"Where is she?"

CJ burst into the waiting room frantically trying to get answers on Asjiah's whereabouts.

Keyshia had called him after the doctors came out and delivered the news, she felt it was only right that he be notified.

"What happened to her? Where is she?"

"CJ calm down."

"Calm down? How the fuck am I supposed to calm down when you told me that she was rushed in here bleeding? Where is the baby? Where is my son?"

"I think we should talk." Mike got up from his chair and approached his friend.

"Talk about what? Everybody keeps saying lets talk but none of y'all muthafucka's are telling me where Asjiah or my son is."

"He didn't make it."

It took a minute for the words to register, for everything to sink in. Mike put his arm around CJ and tried to steady him as his knees became weak.

"No. No. No!"

"They tried but there was nothing they could do, the damage was already done by the time she got here."

"Where is she?"

"Down the hall, room 203. You can't go in there..."

CJ rushed down the corridor almost knocking over the staff that littered the hallways.

"Asjiah,"

Upon entry, he didn't see the boy sitting in the corner until he spoke.

"What the fuck are you doing here?"

"I could ask you the same thing."

"Where the fuck were you at when this shit happened?"

"This here ain't none of your business dude, you can leave now."

"Did you do this to her?"

"What?" CJ began to grow furious with his insinuations.

"Nigga you heard me. Did you do this to her? Why weren't you here when the paramedics brought her in? Why did she call me instead of you?"

Money sat up staring at CJ with daggers in his eyes. He never liked him. He thought he was too soft, a bunch of talk and no action. This was the third time that he knew about in which he had abandoned Asjiah when she needed him. Did he even know she was pregnant, had her miscarriage been caused by his hands? He wanted him gone, out of the picture, the only reason he hadn't laid hands on him was out of respect for Asjiah. For some odd reason she had feelings for the dude so he left him alone, but seeing her in the hospital, being next to her, trying to silence her screams as they announced her baby stillborn, that was too much. He had had enough.

Ignoring Money, CJ approached Asjiah.

"Don't fuckin' touch her."

Money lifted his sweatshirt and flashed the handle of his pistol.

"You don't want to do this here, trust me."

"Excuse me gentlemen, is there a problem?"

Although they were fuming, both tried to appear calm in front of the nurse.

"She's only allowed one visitor at a time, so one of you will have to leave or go to the waiting room."

BY SA'RESE

194

Money sat back down in the chair next to her bed and flicked his hand towards CJ, shooing him away.

CJ was livid; he wanted to punch him in the face until that smug grin disappeared. Who was he to tell him that he shouldn't be here? The tension between them would have to be put to the side for now, Asjiah was in pain and this was neither the time nor the place to settle a childish love triangle. He needed to find out what happened, and who was responsible for the loss of their son.

The scent of marijuana filled the air and circled above her head in ghost like wisps. She kept replaying the day's events over and over in her head hoping that she had been triumphant. The sound of his keys in the door signaled that her love was finally home. She would get to tell him about the sacrifice that needed to be made in order for them to be together, it would probably be a little bit much for him at first, but once he realized the lengths she had gone through, she was sure she would be rewarded.

She took another puff from the blunt, sat it in the ashtray then gave herself a quick straightening before he walked in the door.

"I thought I told you not to come over here anymore." There was no authority behind his words; he was mentally and emotionally drained.

"I missed you."

"Get out of my house Corey."

"You don't really mean that," She offered the joint to him which he reluctantly took.

Inhaling deeply he leaned against the cabinet and tried to clear his head. Disappointment was written all over his face.

STRIPPING ASJIAH

Seizing the moment, she began undressing him. She grew more and more wound up given that he wasn't shunning her advances so she continued to try and massage him into arousal.

The weed was having the desired effect on him that he needed. He wanted to escape what seemed like a terrible nightmare and go back earlier in the week when him and Asjiah were out shopping for baby clothes. He wanted to be with her, to hold her, to feel his son kick beneath his touch.

Reality escaped him and he found himself running his hands through her hair, moaning and saying her name while she performed fellatio on him. on her knees. Ashamed, he pulled up his boxers and fastened his jeans.

"What?"

"Asjiah, you said her name so I asked how she was." Corey relit the blunt and placed the Cannabis between her lips.

"She is in the hospital right?"

"What did you do?"

Corey let out a mischievous laugh, "I did what you couldn't do."

Suddenly he wasn't high anymore; before he knew it he had his hands around her throat.

"What did you do Corrine?"

She smacked his hand and pushed him away from her.

"I killed your little bastard CJ. I did what you wanted to do, but was too scared to follow through on. I did this for us."

He had never put his hands on a female before but when those words escaped her lips, he hit her as if she was a man.

He was crying, weeping inconsolably.

"I did this for us. Why can't you see that?"

He looked into her eyes and saw that she really believed what she was saying. She was crazy. Obsessed, infatuated with

BY SA'RESE

an idea that would never come to fruition, a fantasy that would never be anything more than a delusion, a mirage in her sordid imagination.

"Get out."

"Asjiah."

Even when she was pleasuring him she was still in his thoughts. She couldn't take it anymore, she tried to go about this gracefully and ease him into what she had to say but she couldn't tolerate being in her shadow anymore.

"How is Asjiah by the way?"

The sound of her name brought him back to his kitchen, back to his hardened penis and the sight of Corey

"I'm not leaving this time, you can't make me. I love you, we're in this together."

He left the kitchen and came back with his gun aimed at her head.

"I said get out."

For once, she was quiet. Fear had taken the courage out of her once arrogant demeanor and she was tripping over herself trying to get out of the door.

CJ sat down and put his head on the table. It seemed as though all his scandalous ways, all of his cheating had subsequently led to the unfortunate death of his child.

STRIPPING ASJIAH

Chapter Thirty-Two

"How is she doing?"

Grandma-me held Money's hand gingerly as she thought about her granddaughter.

"She still isn't talking, she won't eat anything and I'm afraid she's only making herself sicker."

Bear whimpered as if he was saddened by Asjiah's current state as well.

Almost five weeks had gone by since she had been released from the hospital and it seemed as though she was sinking further and further into depression.

They both thought it would be a good idea to remove all traces of the baby from the house; they didn't want anything around that would trigger memories or make her upset but when they tried to clean up the nursery Asjiah broke down so they left it as is.

Most days when he would visit, that's where she would be; sitting in the rocking chair, cradling a stuffed animal as if it was a child, staring off into nothingness.

Traces of who she used to be were gone. The bright blue skies that used to be her eyes were now cloudy shades of grey. The smile that was punctuated by deep dimples no longer existed. It was stressful seeing her like this but he wasn't going to give up.

For days he sat with her in the hospital. Night after night she'd awake belligerent demanding to know where baby Jai was, asking the nurses to let her see him, and each time he'd look at her and have to explain what happened which would then result in her crying but he never left; he climbed in bed with her and held her until sadness put her back to sleep.

Eventually the screaming stopped and her pleas turned into silent tears rolling endlessly down her cheeks. He felt as though he was killing her. The constant repetition of his words was like the steady pity pat of bullets piercing her heart.

Angel had told him to watch over her but instead of protecting her he was becoming one of the very people who were tearing her apart. Cannibals like CJ, Cash, Marie, her father; vultures waiting for her to die so they could pick away at her bones. He refused to let that happen, he wouldn't allow her to be consumed by the abyss that was so anxiously waiting to take her away.

Money took to the stairs with Bear following behind him and hoped that today would be a better day, that maybe she would say something or acknowledge his presence.

"Hi pretty girl."

Bear ran up beside her and licked her hand playfully. When she didn't return his affection, he bowed his head and retreated.

"Its okay boy," Money patted the Rottweiler and sent him on his way.

Silence greeted him as usual.

"Caleb told me to tell you what's up."

"…."

"It's a nice day out, not too cold, I figure I can give you a minute to get dressed and we can go out and have a snowball fight."

"…"

Money shrugged and placed his hands in his pockets. "Okay, no snowball fight. What else do you want to do?"

STRIPPING ASJIAH

Her hair looked tangled, tussled in big messy curls that hadn't felt a comb or a brush in who knows how long. She was wearing sweatpants and a wrinkled, Old Navy t-shirt. She was stronger than this. He couldn't continue to sit by and let her whither away.

After rummaging through her closet and dresser drawers, he packed some clothes into a Victoria Secret duffle bag and tossed it down the stairs. He loosened the shoe strings on her all black Air Max 95's and placed them on her feet after putting on her coat and hat.

He knew there was no way she would walk out of here on her own freewill so he picked her up and carried her out to the car.

Grandma-me was in the living room waiting with Asjiah's bag in hand.

Money hugged the lady who he had affectionately named Grandma-C and kissed her cheek.

"Don't worry; I'll bring her back to us."

He hadn't slept in days, weeks since the news had been delivered that his son was dead. How could you be born into this world and die at the same time? He felt as if God was playing some cruel trick on him, punishing him for all the things that he had done in his past. Everything had tumbled so far out of control and he didn't know how to start trying to put things back together.

They were spending more time together, going shopping for the baby, playfully fighting over names, they were getting back to the basics of just having fun.

BY SA'RESE

But its times when you are at your happiest when your past comes back to haunt you and remind you of the things you are trying so hard to forget. In his case it was Corey.

CJ drank straight from the bottle of Hennessey that was sitting to his left then took a drag from the blunt. He couldn't sleep, didn't want to sleep out of dread that everything that had transpired would be waiting for him when he closed his eyes. So instead he tried to find peace in the bottom of a bottle or in the aroma of herbal remedies.

He cleaned his gun and thought of how convenient it was for Money to just materialize out of nowhere and pop up like some kind of fucking genie.

He always appeared at the most favorable moments. He was there when they were on the verge of breaking up last summer, he was there when Asjiah and Angel were almost robbed, and now he was there while she was grieving the absence of their child.

Why did she call Money anyway?

Did she still not trust him? Did she think if she had called him instead that he wouldn't be there for get through this together and in time, when she was ready, talk about starting a family again.

Odd how something so heartbreaking has to take place in order for you to reevaluate what's important to you, one just has to hope that they are able to reconcile before it's too late because time favors no one.

It's true what they say in regards to your life flashing before your eyes when you're about to die, as CJ pulled the receiver back, a single shot rang off and eighteen years went by in seconds.

STRIPPING ASJIAH

her? Whatever the reason, her decision was clear. She chose Money.

He shook his head and grabbed the bottle again.

He tried to go back to the hospital, tried to go visit her but each time Money was there. All he wanted was the opportunity to apologize, to be there for her so they could

Chapter Thirty-Three

Asjiah

The shower poured almost scalding, yet comfortable raindrops over my head.

Anguish was dripping off of me and disappearing down the drain on puffs of hope.

With each tangle he combed through it felt like weeks of sorrow was unraveling and being carried away in streams of conditioner.

He told me he wanted to freshen me up, that he was tired of seeing me in the same clothes, clothes that peeled off of me like extra layers of skin.

I was perfectly still while he undressed me, I watched his eyes ride the curves of my hips, never speeding, taking in every bit of scenery, pausing between golden mountain tops, until finally they rested on lips as sweet as peaches.

But he never touched me inappropriately. Instead he stood behind me in basketball shorts and a t-shirt and lathered my body as if he was waxing an expensive sports car.

He scrubbed my back, squeezing the loofah causing suds to race down my spine slowly trickling down the crack of my ass.

Money got on his knees and took my feet into his hands one by one and washed them the way he had done the rest of me.

He gripped my calf and ascended into heaven rubbing gently over my pearly gates. Sentences from conversations I rehearsed over and over in my head spilled down my thighs intermingling with the creamy body wash. He was making love to me without penetration. Caring for me in a way no one else had.

It wasn't that I didn't appreciate the way he checked on me throughout the week, or that I hadn't noticed how close he had become with Grandma-me, I had become a captive. A hostage within my own mind and I didn't know if I could break free, or if I wanted to.

After he was satisfied with my cleanliness, he wrapped me in a towel and sat me in front of the mirror. He divided my hair with a single part and carefully put it into two fish tail braids. I imagined this is what he did for his grandmother after she developed Alzheimer's.

Not once out of the two weeks that I had been here thus far did he try to kiss me or take advantage of me. Sometimes we would sit in silence for hours and he would hold me until I fell asleep, other days I would watch as he played video games or we would look at ESPN together and he would explain all the various rules of the sports that I didn't understand, but never was he or did he try to be intrusive.

Instead he was patient, thoughtful, and compassionate. He would stare into my eyes and not say a word as if he was silently trying to break me from the asylum that imprisoned me.

It's like I could see all these letters in my brain, but I couldn't make them form words, I couldn't tell him how I felt.

I watched him as he began disrobing. I guess my thoughts were a little too loud because he caught me staring at him and kindly pushed me into the hallway closing the door behind him.

My eyes were transfixed on his chest as water glistened across his body cascading in single drops that skated across his stomach. I wanted to kiss the spot that was still damp behind his ear, to run my tongue across the tattoo that spelled out his alias. I

BY SA'RESE

wanted to give him brain just so I could taste his unspoken thoughts.

I rose from the bed still hugging the towel that veiled my nudity and slowly walked over to him.

"My bad A', I thought you would've been dressed by now. I'll go into the other room."

I intercepted the bottle of lotion he was reaching for and placed it back on the nightstand.

Chills ran across my spine as he placed his hands around my waist.

"What's wrong?"

Timidly I kissed him. My lips grazed his seducing him slowly and for a minute we just stood there breathing. Inhaling and exhaling each other.

Lazily our eyes opened and the yearning in my gaze granted him passage into territory that would take us beyond friends.

The cotton that once provided a barrier between us dropped to the floor and the electricity I felt once our bodies touched ignited a flame in me I didn't know existed.

I felt like I was floating as he placed his palm on the small of my back and laid me down on the plush pillow top. He kissed his way up from my toes, to the back of my knees, then my thighs stopping once he reached my stomach.

He traced the fading pregnancy line that was once proof of a growing fetus and I could tell he shared my pain. In his own way he embodied my loss. I watched his eyes water as I put my hand to his face catching his tears.

Money

STRIPPING ASJIAH

If I tried to explain the way I was feeling I couldn't. I didn't understand it myself but laying here with her, being so close to the spot where a life once lived, it touched me; overpowered me in a way that was beyond my comprehension.

I wanted to take away the hurt, erase her scars and repaint her the way she should be portrayed.

Her skin was so soft, scent so enticing; I've imagined this night so many times, fantasies flooding my daydreams of what it would be like but even while she licks my nipples and my dick gets hard, I push all selfish thoughts to the side, tonight is about deeper, switching up his pace lapping my juices like a kitten does warm milk.

I begin to get butterflies, my breathing becomes rapid. I try to retreat towards the head board only for him to squeeze my ass, place my legs on his shoulders and pull me back into him.

It's like he has a blue print of my body, instinctively he knows where to touch, how much pressure to apply, and suddenly I'm moaning and within seconds he finds that spot again, ravaging it until I explode.

Money

Her desires leave a sticky trail across my face, seems as though I've found my guilty pleasure. A taste I've longed to acquire. I kiss her aggressively as we exchange her desires, allowing her to indulge in her own sweetness.

By the sound of it, I can tell that nigga CJ wasn't hitting it right, she lacks experience; no fault of hers, she just didn't have the right teacher. Her body is tight, untainted like most, fresh clay to be molded within the right hands, my hands.

BY SA'RESE

I'm gentle yet firm enough to get her to submit and allow me to have my way with her.

I kiss her forehead, her cheeks, and then bite the left side of her neck right above her collarbone.

I want to ask but I'm afraid the sound of my voice will bring her back to reality and she may second guess what she's doing. I keep my eyes locked onto hers. I want her to be certain she's ready. I don't want to move too fast.

"Are you sure?"

her.

Asjiah

I gripped the sheets as his tongue parted my lips and excitement dripped onto the bed. He ventures deeper and

Asjiah

I wanted to scream out YES! But instead I simply nod my head in agreement.

I wrap my arms around him; eyes rolling to the back of my head as he enters me.

I take a deep breath, try to hold back and muffle cries of pleasure.

"N'uh uh, let it out."

He sucks on my neck again causing me to whimper sounds of ecstasy.

The heat that's being created between the sheets only heightens our passion as I mimic his movements, thrusting myself into him as he pulls away from me. Our bodies play together like the strings on a violin; a symphony that's been perfectly orchestrated just for us.

STRIPPING ASJIAH

I separate myself from him long enough to disappear under the covers. Intermittently I use my hand more than my mouth, stroking him to the point of ejaculation, allowing him to see the finish line but not reach it.

Not yet.

Money

Fuck.

She's driving me crazy.

Her eyes are drunk with sex, her body high off lust. I reenter her, keeping her flat on her back but positioning her in such a way that we look like scissors.

"I want you to tell me each time you cum, and you bet not stop."

I pull her hair and listen to her whine, the dimples in her back flirting with me each time her ass bounces against me.

Her voice is high pitched, an intense melody that tells me she's about to climax. I feel it too; I pull her closer to me, she quivers as our bodies convulse in rhythmic pulses and we reach bliss together.

Asjiah

Our hearts were in competition with each other. I laid on his chest losing myself in their synchronization, marinating in previous events.

I rolled over on my side so I could look at him under the moonlight. I wanted to apologize for bringing him into this chaos I called my life, to tell him how I truly felt about him but I didn't want him to feel as though I was just sprung off his sex. I needed an expression that would encompass all of my thoughts and as he turned and looked back at me, I said it.

"I love you Jason."

STRIPPING ASJIAH

Chapter Thirty-Four

"I don't want it."

Angel pushed the paper across the table and folded his hands.

"But she would want you to have it. She worked hard to make sure we would be taken care of in case anything happened to her and you're just going to throw it away?"

"I told you, I don't want it."

I folded the letter and placed it in my pocket. I was just as stunned as he was. To know that all this time we were made to believe that we didn't have anything that we had to resort to other means to survive when all the while Marie had this in her possession. Documents that stated we were beneficiaries of individual trust funds that our mother had set up.

Once I realized what I had I visited the lawyer and had everything transferred out of her name into mine. I couldn't touch Angel's account even though I advised him to do the same. I didn't trust her, we had been lied to for this long so who knew what would happen if she remained the primary account holder.

"But Angel-

"It's blood money. Money we inherit only because our mother is dead, money that they feel should be their's because they had to take care of us when in all actuality they haven't done shit but cause us more pain. I've earned my own money. Stood outside on the corner hustling ever since she kicked me out. I don't need it. Fuck them. They can have it."

I didn't want to argue with him. He was getting upset and I didn't want to anger him any further. Instead I would take it and put it away in a safety deposit box, somewhere it would be safe.

"I wish you would've told me about the baby."

"For what? There's nothing you or anyone else could've done to prevent what happened. As cliché as it sounds, everything happens for a reason and I can choose to believe that or drive myself nuts thinking about what I lost."

"I'm just glad you're okay."

I tried to read his face, "Are you okay? I heard about Stacey."

"So," Angel remained poised even though his words were covered in sorrow.

"I know you loved her, I'm so sorry things had to turn out that way."

"It's all for the better, she didn't deserve me anyway."

I was relieved to see him smile, as bad as it may sound; I think he found comfort in her death. That her absence somehow brought him peace and released him from the torment he was feeling. I didn't ask for details pertaining to what happened to her or LT, I knew he would tell me "the less I knew the better" so I left it at that.

"I know you said not to make a big fuss over your birthday but I brought you something."

"What is this?"

I smiled and waited for him to open the envelope.

The sight of her face made him cry, not out of sadness, this time I could tell they were happy tears. Remnants of her were few and far between so when I found this, I knew I had to give it to him.

"Who gave this to you?"

"Grandma-me found it, it was in one of her photo albums."

The picture was of Angel, my mother and I. It looked like it had been shot in a Sears studio. Autumn leaves as the background and her standing beside us with a hand on each of our shoulders. I was maybe all of four which would've made Angel seven at the time.

"All of our memories of her don't have to bring sadness."

"Thank you A', this really means a lot."

I hugged my brother and promised to visit him again next week, "Happy Birthday Angel."

Christmas, a holiday that I lost interest in when my family was dismantled, but thanks to Money, this year would be different.

Grandma-me didn't really do the whole decorating thing but somehow she allowed him to talk her into letting us have a tree. So here we were in the living room, tossing icicles and hanging ornaments, including Bear, who was wearing a Santa hat.

Our relationship had flourished since my "incident", or should I say intensified because it was evident that we always had feelings for each other.

I realized in the time we spent together that what I felt for CJ was merely adolescent infatuation. I never wanted anything from him except loyalty and honesty but he couldn't give me that. I'm not saying that everyday was a bad one because it wasn't; I honestly thought I loved him but when push came to shove I was graciously offered heartbreak and betrayal time after time. I thought we could patch things up, move on and do what was best for our child, but that idea died right along with my baby.

I don't know if he had anything to do with what Corey did to me; I hadn't seen him since Halloween. I heard he moved to Cincinnati, some say he's in jail, he hasn't tried to contact me so I figure, if he really cared, he'd make it known. What I do know

BY SA'RESE

is karma is a bitch. One way or another what goes around comes around.

When I was younger, Angel and I would sneak downstairs at midnight and grab one toy each from underneath the tree, race back up to his room and open them. Of course Angel was absent so that tradition was being reenacted with Money and Grandma-me.

"Here, you first,"

I smiled as she blushed and took the box from me.

"Pooh, you didn't have to get me anything."

"Of course I did."

The rattling of paper made Bears ears stand up and his nub wagged as he waited for her to drop it on the floor.

Her eyes watered and her nose turned red, "Oh my, he's beautiful."

She was holding a silver frame, I had it engraved so it read 'Every Pooh needs a honey pot' and underneath it "Ricordati di me" translated into English meant 'Remember Me' in Italian.

The photo was of baby Jai during the brief time that I was allowed to hold him before he was taken away. At the small ceremony we had for him I asked for a closed casket because it was too much for me to bare, she wasn't able to see him so I knew this photo would mean a lot to her.

I felt a familiar lump in my throat and Money must've picked up on the sudden change of my mood because he handed me my gift next, a jewelry box.

"Open it."

My hands shook as I undid the bow and opened the tiny package. Inside was a necklace with a key on it covered in black and white diamonds.

"It's so pretty!"

"You're not mad are you? Were you expecting a ring?"

"No." I twisted my lips up, this time it was my turn to blush. Money laughed at my all too familiar expression.

"I got something better," He pulled a chain from underneath his sweater. Hanging from his necklace was a safe that matched my charm.

"I had to get something a little more manly, I can't be walking around here with a heart around my neck."

Grandma-me and I giggled at his assertion of testosterone.

"I love it baby."

Before he could open the present I got for him the Ten Crack Commandments erupted from his phone signaling a call from Caleb.

"I'm glad to see you're doing better Asjiah, he's really good for you."

She was the closest thing I had to a mother so her approval of Money really meant a lot to me.

"I think he's good for the both of us."

"What did I miss?" Our chit chat was interrupted with a plate of brownies that he carried in from the kitchen.

I tried to read his face but as usual it was impossible. If there was bad news on the other end of the phone I would never know it. We spent the rest of the evening watching Christmas specials and playing games. Once Grandma-me fell asleep he finally revealed the purpose of the call.

"I have another surprise for you."

"Really, when can I have it?"

"This weekend, we're going out. Make sure to dress for the occasion."

BY SA'RESE

The Metropolis was nestled in the flats of downtown Cleveland. Depending on where you parked you could see the Nautica Queen cruise ship, in the summertime the view of the water was really nice but it was dead Winter and I was cold.

I wasn't really big on going out on New Years Eve but Money had insisted because apparently this was where my surprise was so I donned a black, strapless satin mini dress, and silver sequin stilettos with a matching clutch.

He kept it sexy and simple, dressing in all black with diamonds to compliment his outfit and play off my accessories.

I was a sip away from my third Cranberry and Vodka when he tapped me on the shoulder.

"Your gift is here."

"What?"

He had to pull my dress down for me as I hopped up from the bar stool and looked around.

"Calm down crazy," He laughed in between giving me pecks on the lips. "It's in the bathroom, once you get it, meet me out front."

I was really confused now. My surprise was in the bathroom? Why wasn't it out in the open so everyone could see it? I didn't know whether to ask questions or just follow instructions, I decided on the latter, grabbed my purse and went to the bathroom.

When I entered some Latina girl was standing in the mirror reapplying her makeup practically yelling into a cell phone. It took me a minute to realize the loud mouthed Hispanic chic was Danielle.

I was about to say Hi until she put her finger to her mouth gesturing for me to be quiet. She reached under one of the sinks and handed me a 9mm then pointed towards the stalls.

STRIPPING ASJIAH

A toilet flushed and Keyshia walked out.

Danielle waited for her to wash her hands then both of them left the bathroom.

What the fuck was going on?

And then I heard her.

"Can I get some tissue?"

Three months had passed since my miscarriage and for weeks all I thought about was her. What I would do to her if I ever saw her again, how I would make her pay for what she did. After my grief had subsided she was all I thought about. Money offered a welcome distraction but in the back of my mind she was still there. I had everyone looking for her but to no avail, at least that's what I thought.

So this was my surprise, this was the phone call he had gotten. Somehow Caleb had found her.

"TEN!"

The countdown for the New Year had begun.

"Hello? Is anyone in here? Can a bitch get some toilet paper so I can wipe my pussy?"

I walked toward her voice and stopped in front of the stall.

"NINE!"

"Are you just gonna stand-

I put everything I had into my right foot and kicked the door open; her statement was cut short with the sound of metal hitting her nose.

"Eight!"

"What the fuck?"

Calmly I watched her as she held her hand to her face and blood trickled out of her nostril.

BY SA'RESE

"You thought you could just stomp me out in an elevator and leave me for dead?" I punched her with my free hand and snatched her hair back so she was facing me.

"SEVEN!"

"You thought you could kill my baby and get away with the shit?"

The sound of the gun being cocked echoed through the lavatory.

"Asjiah I…"

BANG!

I stood there and watched the tiny hole in her forehead ooze blood as her pupils dilated.

BANG!

BANG!

"Stop Asjiah, A' stop."

Empty, the gun continued to click as I repeatedly pulled the trigger. Danielle pried the iron out of my hand handing it to Keyshia which she cleaned off then placed into my clutch. Danielle fixed my hair and straightened my dress making sure I looked normal.

We split up, vanishing into the crowd as the final seconds of 2000 ticked off the clock.

Unruffled, I switched to the click clack noise of my heels leading me to the Camry.

As we pulled out of the parking lot Money leaned over and kissed me, "Happy New Year A'."

STRIPPING ASJIAH

Epilogue

Palm trees sway to the summer's breeze as seagulls soar through the sky. The scent of the Pacific Ocean reminds me of days spent on the beach building sandcastles, playing chicken with the waves as they rise to the shore.

I've been here before.

The laughter of innocent children running around on the boardwalk eating cotton candy, trying to hold the gigantic teddy bears they won from aiming water guns at a bull's-eye.

These are my memories being watched from a car window behind a glass that I want to roll down just so I can stick my hand out into the wind with hopes of touching my past.

I wish I could talk to the adolescent me; hold her hand and try to prepare her for what's to come. I'd make her promise that no matter how hard things became that she would always smile. I'd tell her to find a place that she could escape to in her mind that would allow her to hide from the horrors of the world, I'd encourage her to be strong and regardless of what they tell her, as much as they will try to let memories fade, never forget California.

I want to take a detour. Go to the Monterey bay Aquarium, the San Diego Zoo, and Great America. I want to be six again and ride my bike up and down the hills of Thomas Court but I heard the military base we used to live on is no longer there.

I'd like to be anywhere than where I am now.

The landscape is beautiful and the backdrop shows mountain tops making it easy to mistake this place for something else than

BY SA'RESE

what it really is but disassociation won't allow me to distort my reality any longer.

I sign my name along with a series of numbers, empty my pockets and wait for the door to open.

I want to turn around, to go back the way I came and never look back but my steps have already been ordered. Movements calculated, robotic almost.

I walk into another building and it almost feels like I'm in a museum, in some ironic way I guess I am. Looking at statues, formulating my own conclusion of what their lives used to be like before they were sent here. I step into an area the size of a closet and hand my ID to the man behind the gate, another door, last time to turn around.

I enter what looks like a sunroom only larger, vending machines line the walls and tables are scattered across the open space. I find a seat and wait. There's a painting of dolphins on the wall that reminds me of days when I used to go to work with her and watch the untamed waters slam against the rocks, catching an occasional glimpse of a whale diving above the surface. Spanish Bay was my playground.

I pull my sleeves over my hands so that you can barely see my fingers, fold my arms, my leg begins to twitch. Anxiety sets in.

I can't look directly in his face, apprehension won't allow it. I'm scared that I'll drown in seas of blue and drift off with the undertow back to our old house; I'll forget my purpose for being here.

Time has stood still for him or maybe I just kept him frozen in my mind. His skin is the same color of the vanilla ice cream my grandfather used to make. Hair the same rich black as a Raven's feathers, iris's a deeper blue like the waters in Jamaica.

STRIPPING ASJIAH

My hands look like his only smaller. Each mole is in the same spot, each freckle on my face identical to his. I'm a complete replica of his image, the apple of his eye.

I've gone over this moment so many times before, fast forward through all the pleasantries, rewind to replay better days, pressing stop to capture their smiles. I want to mute out the sound; I don't want to hear his voice, afraid that once I press play he'll no longer be the hero I remember but the villain he became.

I can tell he's happy to see me, to him I'm still his baby girl.

He clears his throat.

I look at the exit.

His tone is apologetic, "Asjiah."

"Hello Father."

BY SA'RESE

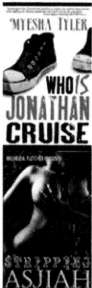

Lá Femme Fatalé Publishing Division
Order Form

Charge it to the Game by Michele Fletcher	$15.95
DC Blood Brothers by Viyo Lance Fire &	$15.95
Flames by Coco	$15.95
Memoirs of a Bitch by Cecelia Robinson	$12.95
Stripping Asjiah by Sa'Rese	$15.95
Stripping Asjiah II Blood Money by Sa'Rese	$15.95
Taka by Tyberia Blaqk	$15.95
Taka II Unfinished Business by Tyberia Blaqk	$15.95
No Witnesses by Rochelle Magee	$15.95
Who is Jonathan Cruise by Myesha Tyler	$15.95
The Preacher's Daughter by Kendra Dunn	$15.95
No Witnesses II By Rochelle Magee	$15.95
Bliss by K.D. Harris	$15.95
Bliss II by K.D. Harris	$15.95
Playgound by K.D. Harris	$15.95
Derailed by D.Skies	$15.95
Vexed by Les Jones	$15.95
Street Covenant by Latanya L. Jones	$15.95

Shipping/handling (via U.S. Priority Mail)
$4.05 per Book   Total $_____

Purchaser Information

Name: _____ Reg #: _____
Address: _____
City: _____ State: _____
Zip:_____ Total Number of Books Ordered: _____

For orders shipped directly to prisons Lá Femme Fatalé Productions deducts 25% off the sale price of the book. Costs are as follows: Shipping/handling $4.05 Lá Femme Fatalé Productions 9900 Greenbelt Road, Suite E-333 Lanham , MD 20706 1-866-50-femme (33663) www.lffpublishing.com